I0566539

The Newfoundland Vampire Book III

"The Gathering Dark"

By

Charles O'Keefe

Newly-made vampire Joseph O'Reily has rejected his vampire lover Cassandra and declared their relationship at an end. Although he loves Cassandra – and she loves him – he knows their relationship cannot survive because she places such low worth on human life and morals.

Former pirate and vampire sire Anne Bonny is bored from spending almost a century on a tropical island and makes her way to St. John's after receiving the last thoughts of her creation, John Snow. Once in Newfoundland she engages with Joseph and Cassandra, both of them surprised to see a vampire that doesn't wish them harm.

Joseph, who is dealing with his failed relationship with Cassandra and his new one with Anne, has forgotten a human figure from his past, Augustus Green, a pimp and murderer. Green plans revenge for the brutal beating Joseph and Cassandra gave him months ago.

The Emperor Commodus, leader of the vampire council, has commanded his subjects, Count Dracula, Countess Elizabeth Bathory and others, to swell the ranks of his evil army by creating brainwashed vampires. Hope is not lost though as other vampires secretly prepare for the war to fight for their survival and humanity's.

Anne Bonny devises a plan that would mean the death of the Countess and replacing her. Joseph must make the decision to join Anne on his own. As his enemies gather, so do his friends, and Joseph discovers he has allies he never even knew about. The good side of the Council holds its own meeting that Joseph and Cassandra are secretly invited to.

With Anne and Cassandra at his side, they wage a desperate battle against the Countess, in the hopes of not just defeating her but striking a pre-emptive blow against the forces of evil. Joseph is ready to take on his greatest challenge yet. If he wins, good will prevail. If he fails, he will enable the destruction of the entire world. With a lot riding on him, Joseph can only hope for help from old friends and old flames alike, if he is to turn the tide of destiny.

THE NEWFOUNDLAND VAMPIRE

BOOK III

THE GATHERING DARK

by

Charles O'Keefe

Copyright 2016 Charles O'Keefe

Licensed and Produced through
Four Phoenixes Publishing
United States Canada United Kingdom

PRINTED IN USA
PRINT ISBN/EAN-13: 978-0-9976205-4-2
Cover art by Kevin Kendall, Kendallight Studios
www.kendallightstudios.com

~ACKNOWLEDGEMENT AND DEDICATION~

First off I want to thank my wife, Joanne, for all her love and support. It sounds corny but she completes me, I couldn't imagine my life without her and I love her more every day.

I want to thank all the fans for their patience. Three years is a long time for a new book, I won't bore you with excuses, life happens. I'm self-published (with some other wonderful authors on a team) and it's an exciting time for me, I'm learning a lot and while I can't guarantee I'll stay with this method, I'm certainly giving it a try. That said I'd like to promote my group, Four Phoenixes Publishing, and I hope when you're done with this book you'll consider reading other great novels by Jennifer L. Gadd, Joe Chianakas and TP Keane.

I've worked with six different editors (you know who you are) and I'd like to thank them all for being instrumental in showing me how to become a better writer (it's a life-long process). You all indirectly made this book a much better story. I also had some early input from Lisa Daly and I'd like to thank her for that, along with her husband Shannon Green. His rather unsavory character plays an important role in this book and I thank him for being a good sport about it, it has been fun to write such a nasty fellow and I want to make clear the real Green is (almost) nothing like him. I want to thank Colin for a clarification of a police procedure. My friend John for always being a great sounding board and my parents for always believing in me and encouraging my writing. Someone I should have mentioned before is Darrell Heath for his help formatting this print copy.

His continued support with my website and promotional materials is much appreciated.

I also want to thank Kevin Kendall for his wonderful cover artwork. He was very accommodating to my specific ideas and a pleasure to deal with. He lives here in Newfoundland (though not next to me) and I encourage you to check him out at Kendallight Studios on the web.

Life is strange, the older you get the more often you look back on what you're done. I'm proud of my Newfoundland Vampire series and I hope you're enjoying it. If you haven't read book 1 and book 2 (Killer on the Road) I would highly encourage you do so before you read this. That said this is not the end, book four as I write this has been about half-written, so expect in to come out sometime in the next year or
so.

Until then I'll leave you with a quote from my favorite song, listen to it and let it teach you about life, death and happiness. "Somewhere between the time you arrive and the time you go, may lie a reason you were alive, but you'll never know." Jackson Brown, "For a Dancer."

Charles O'Keefe
July, 2016

The Newfoundland Vampire

Book III

"The Gathering Dark"

By

Charles O'Keefe

Prologue

My Bonny Lies Over the Ocean

Anne Bonny sat on the beach of Green Island, Hawaii, sipping a mai tai as she admired the view of the sunset. The sky began to turn crimson red, which helped dull the intense headache she suffered as a vampire up before dark.

She resided near what was thought to be an abandoned Coast Guard station, which secretly harbored her underground mansion and several paid servants and guards. Underneath a run-down airstrip lay a subterranean waterway where a submarine was docked. The submarine was used primarily for the human servants that needed to leave the island to fetch supplies or take vacations.

Anne, like many vampires, was quite wealthy. Wise investments over enough time provided financial comfort that most well-to-do humans accumulated only through inheritance, corporate sharking, or a serendipitous blend of ideas, timing, and networking. Like most vampires, Anne chose not to flaunt her wealth. It was easier to hide from humans that way. Peace and quiet was easy to obtain on a deserted island.

Anne shifted in her chair. *Life is like a box of chocolates, you never know what you're going to get.* She laughed to herself at the reference—that was a good movie. She began to softly sing, "My bonny lies over the ocean; my bonny lies over the sea..." She liked that song, even though it wasn't about her. As she sang and took another sip from her drink, she closed her eyes and grimaced in pain. Her estranged youngling John, currently thousands of miles away, was in

1

terrible danger and perhaps faced death. Despite the pain, she smiled and reclined easily on her lounger.

Serves the bastard right, Anne thought. *His charms fooled me, and I made him one of us. It's time his life was brought to an end.*

Anne sighed, and as the sun dipped near the horizon, her pounding headache and aching limbs eased up. Anne thought of that spring day in 1834. John was a handsome man who exuded charisma and confidence. A hundred and thirty years had gone by so fast. Time was relative when one was immortal. Newfoundland had fit the pirate lifestyle for so long – Peter Easton, Black Bart, and George Fielding all had frequented the area in years gone by. She'd enjoyed her life as a pirate. She loved to capture booty, but didn't delight in slaughter.

Anne took another sip of her drink and concentrated. John was fortunate that the sun was about to set, and her powers activated in time.

A man in a white shirt and shorts came over to her. "Excuse me, mistress. May I get you another drink?"

Anne opened her eyes. "No, Charles, I'd like to be alone. Take away the glass and bring me my cell phone in a bit."

The man nodded. "As you wish." He took the glass and left.

Anne resumed her concentration, and John entered her mind fully. *Anne, my death is moments away, my own youngling Catherine and this motherfucker Joseph are the cause. If you ever cared for me, avenge my death. I am in Newfoundland, and I will give you my last images so you will know their faces.*

Anne snorted and thought back, *Go fuck yourself, John. Just die already!*

Anne received no reply, but an image formed in her mind. She was in some kind of park, with trees and a pond nearby. Blood poured from wounds around the stomach and another from the throat. Anne was experiencing John's last moments, his moment of death. There was a statue of Peter Pan, animals around the feet, and a lot of blood on the ground. There was a woman with beautiful long red curly hair who was terribly wounded in her chest, and man with a bloody shoulder and missing teeth who stabbed John with a sharpened wooden stick.

Anne gasped as her own chest hurt terribly for a second. And then she received one final thought from John. *They watch us.*

Anne waited for the pain to fade and rubbed her chest right above her heart. She snorted again and grumbled to herself, "Tell me something I don't know."

With the sun gone down, she sat up and smiled, absently admiring her slim, athletic figure in her gold bikini. She tossed back her own fiery red hair, kept straight and at shoulder length.

"My dear John," she said aloud, "your death, and these other vampires in Newfoundland, pique my interest."

The last remnants of the sun disappeared below the horizon, and Anne felt her senses fully come to life. Charles' heartbeat thumped in her ears and she smelled the sweetness of his blood. As he approached, she stood and held out her hand for the phone.

Charles said in his accustomed manner, "Are you hungry, mistress?" He passed her the phone and stretched his neck to one side.

Anne smiled.

Charles nodded. "Thank you for choosing me tonight."

Anne took the phone and clipped it on the back of her bikini bottom. She took off Charles' shirt and sank her teeth into his neck. He tasted lovely with not a hint of drugs or alcohol and a pleasant taste of cinnamon in his blood. She drained Charles until his heartbeat started to slow and he drifted into unconsciousness. Anne cared for her servants, the way a pet owner cared for her animals, and she laid him gently on the sand.

She took the cell phone out and punched in the mansion number. She didn't allow time for a greeting but simply stated, "Have a boat waiting on the southeastern end of Midway Island. I'll whistle. Also, prepare the sub and head off for Honolulu. I'll be there in a few days. Make sure it has my weapons on board. Oh, and send Michael down to take Charles to sickbay. He'll need a few days off."

The reply came instantly. "Of course, mistress, right away."

Anne tucked the cell phone into Charles' right front pocket and, after a brief glance at the sky, dived into the ocean. The water was warm against her cool skin. It would take her weeks to get there this way, but she was in no rush. Anticipation was an exquisite thing, and time was certainly on her side.

Part 1:

Breaking up is hard to do

Chapter 1: *And the meek shall inherit . . .*

Joseph returned from his walk, his new cat, Jude, in his arms. Once again, loneliness pressed into his mind. The last few weeks felt pointless, he was alone again. Life before Cassandra had been lonely, with little to no dealings with women. He'd been shy, awkward but ready for a change. That change had come in Cassandra. She was the woman of his dreams and while at first the shock of becoming a vampire was extreme, he now saw he'd wanted it. Who could turn down power, immortality, and eternal youth?

But Cassandra had turned out to be a lot different than he had thought. Her capacity for violence, the lies, and most importantly, her disregard for human life, all too much for him to handle. He had had to let her go and had just broken up with her a couple of hours ago. She was his sire and the connection was so strong, even now he felt her presence, like a warm strumming song in his head, even though she was miles away.

He sighed, and Jude brushed his head against Joseph's chest, purring, closing his eyes and meowing. The poor guy was no doubt hungry and Joseph had to stop wallowing in self-pity and sadness, at least for the moment. He went inside and put Jude in the bathroom, so he could take care of Ginger. She had already hissed at Jude once and he didn't want to deal with it anymore tonight. He took care of both cats separately, cleaned Jude up and gave him a flea treatment.

He lay down on his bed and Jude climbed up the blankets to lie with him. He absently stroked the cat's head and reflected on his life over the past few weeks. Only six weeks since his whole life had changed. He was quite literally a new man; not even human. He had learned that vampires existed, Cassandra was one, he was now one, and that many others skulked around the world. His childhood idol, William Shatner, was one and evil figures like Elizabeth Bathory and Hitler still caused death and destruction as vampires.

A sound at the window started him, and he sat up, dislodging Jude, who glared up at him. It was nothing, a moth drawn by the light of his bedroom, and he lay back again. Was he always going to be afraid? He was a vampire-he shouldn't be so scared all the time. But he had seen so much evil, from vampires and human, that he didn't know how he could return to any semblance of normal life. His quiet, sheltered world was forever shattered.

He got up and made himself a strong drink. His parents always had a well-stocked liquor cabinet and he was glad that at least booze still had the same effect. He had known so much hate in others, had seen the suffering it caused and the deaths. Cassandra had shown him a world of monsters hidden just below the surface of society. She had shown him cruelty and her disregard for human life had disgusted him. More than all of that he felt repulsed by himself, by his inability to stop the deaths of innocent people. There was that woman, Jennifer that he—rather *they*—had let die. How he drank her blood. He polished off the whisky, grimaced and poured himself another. The taste was strong but he gulped down the golden liquid.

Another innocent who died, the woman Donald had captured and Cassandra had killed. So much death, so much pain. There was James, the shooter in the theater during a screening of Batman. Maybe he would have faced the death penalty but Cassandra didn't have the right to kill him. The savage beating they gave him was enough.

He slammed back the rest of the second glass and felt the warm tingling of alcohol spread over his body. He put the glass down and lay back down on the bed once more. He smiled. There was that Green guy; they had beat the shit out of him, but he deserved it. Joseph hoped he would rot in jail for a long time. He chuckled as he remembered meeting Shatner and how his worry had turned to delight when he discovered that he was also a vampire. If anyone could help the world, he was sure Shatner, and whoever else was on the good side of the Council, could.

The booze was hitting him and he let it. His eyes drooped and he drifted off.

* * *

Joseph put on his coat and slung his book bag over his shoulder. He had such a terrible day that he didn't even care that his coat was on inside out. It was almost five and he had spent the last two hours with a teacher going through the mistakes he had made in his English paper. He'd had a crappy day. He kicked the door open and went outside. Today, like many days, he wished he was something other than human. He wished he had special powers.

At that moment he had the strangest sensation; it was almost as if someone tugged at this mind. It felt like someone else had somehow spied on his last few thoughts. He shook his head to clear it. He was just tired; telepathy was only in stories. He saw his mom in the other end of the parking lot and slowly headed towards her.

At least I have role-playing this weekend. An escape to a fantasy world helped him deal with reality and he took that escape whenever he could.

Just before he reached the car, scratching and a meow caught his attention. He called out to his mom, "I'll be right over; I think I hear a cat." She waved at him and he assumed that meant she understood. He went toward the

The Newfoundland Vampire   Charles O'Keefe

wooded area near the school. A few years ago he would play in these woods with his friends and by himself. A paper bag moved slightly on the ground just ahead of him. A small cat clawed its way out of the bag. Joseph grinned. He picked up the cat and held her to his face. She purred and rubbed against him, happy to be free. He had always loved animals, cats in particular, and he instantly felt the desire to love and care for this cat.

The leaves moved for just for an instant and he heard a small snap nearby. He thought he caught a glimpse of red hair glinting in the sunlight. For an instant he considered investigating who it was, but a car horn and the cat next to him meowing snapped him back to the present. He turned and proudly brought the cat over to his mom. His love of animals and fantasy remained but soon he had a new obsession. Vampires.

* * *

He awoke from the dream to find Ginger batting at his lip. He called out "Uhh, what?" and gently brushed her away. The sun had not quite set and his head was pounding. Jude took this moment to pounce on Ginger from behind the door and the calico cat made a strangled meow and ran off. He lay back down and rubbed his temples. Jude climbed up on the bed once more and kneaded his chest. *When I was thirteen, was it Cassandra that started my obsession with vampires? Maybe gave it a nudge and fostered its growth?*

It did make sense; she knew that she would turn him someday and made certain the desire was there, though it was always something he had wanted. He would confront her about it. But not right now, right now he wanted to focus on something else. He would take care of the cats and head to campus. Mark, his psychic fill-in from a week ago, had left a schedule by his bed and if he hurried he could make his philosophy class.

As he headed out the door there was a small "ping" sound. He pulled his phone out of his pocked and flicked his finger across the screen. Opening up his e-mail he found it, "Negative consequences of Soy milk", he rolled his eyes, *from Mom, of course.* Since he had become vegetarian she lectured him about it.

Now it's just funny. He laughed and opened the e-mail. *Don't drink too much of this stuff. It mimics estrogen and isn't good for you! Also remember we'll be home in a few days. Love you and we'll see you soon.*

"Shit!" Joseph slammed his fist into his leg, his phone slipped out of his right hand and he just got his left up in time to catch it. *As if I don't have enough going on, totally forgot they will be home soon. Life is going to get even more complicated.* He jumped in the car and sped off.

* * *

Anne Bonny swam quickly through the frigid waters of the Atlantic Ocean. She barely recognized the cold but the seaweed, garbage, fish and occasional whale could not be ignored. Swimming for almost eight hours taxed even a vampire body and she needed a break. Green Island, her Hawaiian island home, was a long ways off but she had enjoyed the stop in Honolulu. That local man was so large, he was full of tasty blood, spicy and exotic, and the sex wasn't bad either. Then she'd rested in Yarmouth, Nova Scotia last night, a tiny town, quaint but boring to tears. At least finding a woman for the night had proved an enjoyable challenge.

As she surfaced and spit out the salty water, she saw the large ferry pulling away from the dock. North Sydney was another tiny town but as far as she could make it tonight. The dockyard smelled of gasoline, oil and salt and it made her grimace. She stopped breathing and dove under the water just before the wave from the ferry could hit her.

Somehow under the surface was better. She swam at full speed and blurred through the water, too fast for any marine life to observe. She ripped through the water and soon reached the dock. Once more pulling off kelp, seaweed and a dead fish, she climbed up the wooden indentations on the side and made her way onto the dock. Realizing people might spot her, she started to breathe and her breath puffed out before her in the chilly air. The pavement was hard beneath her feet and she wanted to get out of her wet, cold underwear. A tall chain link fence was just in front of her, she turned her head from side to side, then took a few steps back and somersaulted gracefully up and over it. Her wet hair was in her face and she wrung it out a little and pushed it back with her fingers. She reached out with her senses but could find no other vampires.

The smell of a human was close, however, and she smiled. *I do need some clothes and a lift to the casino, after all.*

A man with shaggy brown hair and a thick moustache approached immediately. Apparently an attractive woman walking around in a bikini with something strapped to her back was hard to miss.

"Hello?" he called out. "This isn't a public area."

Anne smiled wickedly and licked her lips. "That's fine, my dear, because you found me at your car and I looked so cold you gave me your overalls and all the cash on you."

The man blinked and lowered his arms. He reached inside his pocket and mechanically got his car keys, deactivating the lock. "My truck is just over here. Come in before you catch your death."

Anne hurried up to him and kissed him on the cheek. "Oh, how kind of you, good sir. I hope you have someone to go home to and keep you warm."

The man blushed. "Oh…um…no, but I do have a dog."

Anne quickly helped him out of his overalls and took the $200 from his wallet. She couldn't help but stare at the Canadian money; it was plastic and so brightly colored, odd indeed.

Drop me off at the casino, if you don't mind. She mentally reinforced to him, *you never saw me, you went to the casino and had some bad luck, you left your overalls there too since they wouldn't let you wear them inside.*

As he dropped her off, Anne glanced about. It was dark and dreary, flurries had started to come down just a little. She squeezed the rest of the water from her hair and ran her fingers through it. *Some more money in my pocket and I'll have a fine enough evening. Tomorrow I'll spring for the ferry and in the evening I'll find Cassandra.*

She laughed and sauntered into the casino.

Chapter 2: Separate Ways

Joseph took care of the cats and separated them by putting Ginger outside. It was a cool night, but it wasn't snowing, and he would certainly be back before morning. He put his cutlass in the trunk; he knew better than not to have it with him. Cassandra, while he may not agree with her morals, had given him valuable lessons and he had taken them to heart.

He was a creature of habit, and in some sense, he relied on them. They made his life familiar and gave him a sense of normalcy. Heading to class on a Monday night felt right and he let out a sigh of contentment. He plugged in his iPod and put it on shuffle. As luck would have it, the first song made him reflect on Cassandra.

I don't wanna lose you,
I don't wanna use you
Just to have somebody by my side

Cassandra, he couldn't quite figure her out. He loved to be with her. She was good to him, sexy as all hell, dynamite in bed, affectionate but not clingy, and she genuinely loved him. The problem, as the song said, was that "sometimes love just ain't enough." He just couldn't live with what she was capable of, what she had done to the Batman wacko and Donald's hostage. More than anything, he feared what he would become if he stayed with her.

The song ended and Joseph sped up as the car ploughed into the clear fall night. His senses alive, he rolled down the window and breathed in the fresh air. His sense of smell as a vampire was so much stronger than as a human. The thickness of the trees, the acridness of the car exhaust, the horrible smell of a dead rabbit on the side of the road, even the faint whiff of animal droppings from somewhere in the trees all drifted toward his nose.

Perhaps this is why dogs like to stick their heads out of car windows. It certainly was a feast for his senses.

As Cassandra had taught him, he began to eliminate noises and scents. First the exhaust fumes, then the road kill, followed by engine noises and the tires, until he was left with just the wind and the smells of nature. It was a relaxing, peaceful presence, and he closed his eyes, for just a split second. With his heightened reflexes he found his body told him what to do and he could almost drive this route blindfolded, he knew it so well.

Thank you Cassandra. You taught me well.

He'd meant to think that to himself but that wasn't how vampire minds worked. He opened his eyes wide. He knew what would come next, because with a sire and progeny even a glancing thought of each would be heard, unless he was careful to lock his mind up first.

A second later he felt her presence, close, at Memorial University, maybe attending a class herself. She entered his mind. *You're welcome, my love. Remember, I'll always be here if you need me.*

He nodded and swallowed. The temptation would always be there. He pulled into the parking lot and sighed once more. He did the mental trick of sealed his thoughts up and said aloud, "I know you always will, but I have to be strong."

He collected his books, put them in his backpack, locked the car and headed off. It was colder out in St. John's than at home and, as a human, he might have taken the tunnels that connected all the buildings, but now it didn't matter. He took his time walking through campus. Just a few weeks ago he had rushed back to Cassandra's room here on campus, happy and excited, only to lose himself staring at his hand and the way everything was illuminated with a faint green glow. He needed to get back there somehow, recapture the magic that the world had held when he was a young vampire full of piss and vinegar.

He chuckled to himself at that saying. It didn't make much sense.

The Arts building was now on his right and he turned to enter. *You just need time.* He remembered a movie that said you needed half the time you dated to get over them and move on. He had only met Cassandra six weeks ago, so if it took three weeks to get back to himself, so be it. He did, after all, literally have an eternity.

He ventured into the classroom and took his seat. It was Dr. Locke's class again, and this time the focus would be on love, rather than morality. Someone had written love on the whiteboard ahead of time and had surrounded it with hearts and even an adequately drawn cupid.

Dr. Locke chuckled at it as he entered the room and went to erase it but then stopped. "As at least one astute and artistic person has noted, tonight we will be talking about love. More precisely, Plato's definition of it as was taught to him by Socrates."

Joseph opened his notebook. At least he'd have something to think about for the next few hours other than Cassandra.

Locke continued, "A lot of you most likely know the term Platonic love and no doubt think of this as love for a friend or family member, the kind that doesn't include a sexual connection. This definition, however, is not what Plato meant."

Joseph sat up in his chair. Locke, ever observant, nodded at him and continued. "In the fifth century C.E. when Plato wrote much of his works, his conception of love was about two men. Men and women's only purpose together was procreation, a notion that he certainly would have changed had he lived in more modern times."

Joseph scribbled down some notes as Locke continued. "Plato begins with the idea that love is connected to the concept that we are incomplete. We strive for our other half, if you will, but much more than that we look for goodness. This drive fuels us and while we may never obtain pure goodness, it's something which we want to eternally possess."

A student in the front raised his hand. "So if I spent the rest of my life searching for the best, purest, tastiest bottle of scotch, I would be considered in love with scotch and in pursuit of good?"

Locke chuckled as did some of the other students. "Well, if you recognize the goodness in a fine bottle of liquor you could be on a path to completeness. He would say though that you need to ultimately connect with other likeminded philosophers and perhaps share that bottle together."

Joseph liked that idea, the search for completeness and the pursuit of the good. *What does it mean to be good? Can I ever live up to an ideal as a vampire? What would complete me? Is it another person? Would I be better off a lonely hermit, mediating on some mountaintop in the Himalayas, waiting for Bruce Wayne to show up so I could train him?*

He smiled to himself. He had an eternity to search for both and perhaps one day he would create another like him, someone who would encourage him to be better, not to drag him down.

Locke glanced at his watch. "Well I'm currently in pursuit of a good cup of coffee. I'll see you all back here in ten minutes."

Joseph got up, grabbed his knapsack and went outside. He was enjoying the class but his nature was pulling at him. All these heartbeats, veins pulsing, blood pumping, called to him and tried to pull him away from his good intentions. He quickly hurried past a few smokers outside and walked around to the side of the building. He took in deep breaths and concentrated. He could make it through the rest of the class. This was the return to normalcy that he needed right now.

He reached out with his senses, not intentionally searching for Cassandra but checking for another vampire nonetheless. He found Cassandra, so close. Well she had as much right to be here as he did and it was a comfort to know if something did go wrong, as it had many times since he started this strange vampire life, at least she would be there to help.

* * *

Cassandra felt him. Joseph was searching for another, just checking she imagined, and found her. *I'll be here, dear one, at least for now.* While she didn't agree with his overly righteous morality, she could understand it. In his mind and soul he still felt so human. He hadn't lived through what she had: wars, death, destruction, atrocities. The human race had not shown its true nature to him yet.

Not that she was filled with hatred and bitterness, some humans she quite liked, but vampires could use their experiences and wisdom to dish out justice. Some people only wanted to hurt others and cause pain and the world was better off without them.

Her mind drifted back toward the professor and the class. It was a class on the ideas of the media, propaganda and the treatment of women in society. Joseph would likely have enjoyed it. The professor was soft-spoken but energetic and wanted feedback from the students, something Cassandra appreciated. Tonight a discussion on the inequality of wages for women had moved onto the issues surrounding maternity leave.

"Many aspects of society are predisposed to put women down. In the United States right now many people feel that the health care system treats pregnancy as a disease and therefore childbirth as the cure to this disease."

Cassandra mulled this over as murmurs spread throughout the classroom. *That's a bizarre notion. Pregnancy is a natural part of life, not a disease. I had eight children and while most of the births hurt like hell, I always considered my children a huge part of my human life, though they did make working difficult at times.*

Professor Hill continued and Cassandra listened. She never bothered to take notes. She liked to reflect on anything said in class and if it was interesting or important to her, she would study it further.

As she left the class she once more thought of Joseph and sighed. She did miss Joseph. He approached everything with such a unique view and could always make her laugh. At the same moment she felt his presence, so near, just a few buildings over. It would be so easy to send him a message, even to go to him, but she would not. Perhaps someday he would come back to her, but he needed to make that decision on his own. She owed him that much.

She would retrieve her sword from her locker and walk downtown. Perhaps she could find a person to drink from and, if nothing else, she wanted to smell the salty air and look out at the harbor. *Why do things never work out for with love? With John I was young and stupid but the others, Tobias and Arthur, good men I loved and loved me back. I was so obsessed with getting rid of John that I didn't even think of the consequences of having them murder him and of course back then I had no idea what John had become.*

She walked through the tunnel at Memorial which connected the science building to many other around campus. Quickly finding the stairs up to the Arts and Administration building she headed up. While outside was quicker she wanted a little more time to think, some solitude. *The only useful thing John ever did was make me strong, he showed me the savage nature of man and what it takes to survive.* Climbing three flights of stairs took her a few minutes, she took her time. *Did John's lesson make me cruel? Jaded to the suffering of others and the fate of humans? Was the emotional wall I build up around me too hard for Joseph to climb?* Reaching her locker at the skywalk she began to turn the numbers. *Joseph took me years to find and I watched him, even encouraged him to love vampires.* She pulled open the door of her locker and quickly put her sword inside her coat, with vampire speed even a camera would only record it as a blur. *Maybe I was wrong about Joseph, his genteel nature was simply no good for vampire life. I'll always love him, he is my blood, a descendant of the child I had without John but he needs to find his own way in the world and I'm done wallowing in sadness.* Closing the locker and re-locking it she cleared her mind and strode forward, back down the stairs and into the night air.

* * *

After a long trip on the ferry, Anne arrived in Newfoundland. She got on the Harley she had arranged to be waiting for her. She was tired of public transportation and wanted to feel the wind in her hair. It was a cold, windy, foggy night but it didn't bother her. Her enhanced senses warned her of any wildlife that might run onto the highway and the weather reminded her of Ireland.

She was pulled over twice for not wearing a helmet but it was nothing a little vampire telepathy couldn't handle. "Oh,

I'm an American, from Colorado, we don't have helmet laws there."

That one made her smile. She laughed at the second time she was pulled over just outside Whitbourne. "*Ní féidir liom labhairt Béarla.*" The man scrunched his eyes together and scratched the side of his head. He obviously didn't speak Galic and had no idea how to explain what she had done wrong. She just wiped his mind and sped off before he even had a chance to reply.

With the exit off the highway just ahead, she pulled over to the side of the road and concentrated. Closing her eyes, she extended her senses and was please to find not one, but two vampires, only a few miles away.

"Ahh, Catherine, you and your boy toy are still here. Good." The hunger in her belly gnawed at her, she put her hand on the throttle and got the bike in motion.

* * *

Anne pulled her motorcyle up onto the sidewalk on the corner of George and Adelaide streets. A sign read *Holdsworth Court.* She parked her bike around the corner, out of sight of most people. A ticket didn't bother her but having the bike towed would be a nuisance. She made sure her sword was strapped to her back and not obvious under her jacket. She had read about George Street on her phone, it was a tiny spot, but had the highest concentration of bars in a two block radius of any place in North America. The fact that it was closed to cars should also make her stroll more enjoyable.

It was ten p.m. and the streets had very few people about. Coming from just ahead of her was music and talking, but much more interesting was the tantiziling smell of blood and cacphony of heartbeats. She sauntered up the street and went into the first place she saw, a dark blue building called *Kelly's Pub*. A few eyes turned towards her as she entered, and the bouncer at the door gave her a curious glance, then nodded at her.

Once inside, she immediatiely saw the appeal of Newfoundland. The bartender smiled at her and said, "It's ladies' night, drink are free 'til midnight." She smiled back but mostly stared at the vein on the bartender's neck that pulsed and throbbed with delicious blood.

"Ahh, lovely," Anne replied. "I'll have a double rum and coke."

Sipping her drink, she scanned the room. A few women sat further down at the bar, about ten men lounged about, most in their 40s but a couple in their 20s. A band was slowly setting up on stage and Irish music played over the speakers.

Spring's a girl from the streets at night,
Dirty old town, dirty old town.

Anne smiled. It was a catchy tune and she certainly was on the prowl. A man approached her, he had a gait, a strut where he leaned from one side and then the other, and he almost slid across the floor towards her. *He was confident, or at least did a good job faking it.* He was tall, handsome but had a tattoo that ran up his neck along with a large round plug in his earlobe, so much the pity.

He smiled back at her. "Hey there, get you another one of those?"

She smiled back and immediately started to work her telepathy on him. She wasn't in the mood to be hit on by a local who probably was only after one thing.

"Sure. When in Rome, as they say. I'm Anne, you?"

He motioned to the bartender who poured her up another rum and coke.

He had a swig of his beer before replying, "Oh, I'm Mark, nice to meet—"

Cutting him off, she entered his inebriated mind while she downed her drink in one motion. *You'll meet me outside around the back. Pay off your tab first, you won't be coming back.*

Mark blinked and laid a hand on her shoulder. "I'll see you in a minute."

Anne went outside. She was a little dismayed—there wasn't a behind to this bar, it was adjoined to another building. Nonetheless, a green and white chip truck would provide a little cover.

Mark stumbled out onto the patio, finished his drink and soon spotted her. She let him kiss her for a moment but the garlic, beer, and bread on his breath soon ended that. She wrapped his mind up in a trance and buried her head inside his puffy winter jacket, sucking his blood and obtaining that connection vampires crave. As always, she finished just as he passed out and after relieving him of his cash, she used his cell phone to call the police. She knew he owed a fortune in traffic fines and she was sure the cops would be happy to have him. She wrapped his coat around him and put on his hat, leaving him propped against the wall of the club and easy to spot. She certainly didn't want him to freeze to death.

Wiping her lips and smiling, she checked her sword, and began to whistle as she walked down Holdsworth Street and toward Duckworth Street. She reached out with her senses and found another, so close, only one or two miles away. She hoped it was Catherine. She had had enough of men tonight and was ready to meet this redhead from John's last moments of life.

* * *

Cassandra left Memorial University, walking slowly and trying to enjoy the night. She missed Joseph but his mind was made up, at least for now. Perhaps in time he would come back to her, would need her again, but for now she would manage on her own. She headed down Allandale Road, the quickest way to get downtown, and did her usual search for another, only expecting to find Joseph.

To her surprise and trepidation, there was another. Close, perhaps two miles away and somewhere downtown. Instinct made her reach inside her jacket to ensure that her sword was there. It was a small comfort as she weighed her options. She could contact Joseph— despite what had happened, she knew he would help.

She reconsidered and didn't reach out to him, as this person was not actively seeking her out, not at the moment at least. She would leave Joseph alone. If this was another member of the cursed council perhaps she could spare him from it. In any case, she was curious. Not all vampires wanted to kill each other and perhaps this one was just passing through.

She would head out to Signal Hill. At least there among the cliffs there would be no chance of anyone getting hurt and it was a spot she would even like to show a visitor. She straightened her back and shoulders and quickened her pace. *Whoever you are, I'm ready for you. You'll find a Newfoundland Vampire is not something to be taken lightly.*

Chapter 3: Female Companionship

Cassandra walked quickly, not running, but with purpose. New Gower Street soon became Military Road and then Signal Hill Road. She couldn't run, after all, even if it was ten at night on a Monday in October. Even with empty streets someone could still be at a window.

She reached back to make sure her sword was still there. She checked the front of her belt for her throwing knives and the back of her pants for the gun. She had never liked guns but after having to fight Thomas, John, Donald's imposter, and Donald himself, all in the span of a month, she'd had a change of heart and would carry one for now.

She walked up the hill past houses and the Battery Hotel. The road was steep and the ground was slippery from all the rain. The wind whipped at her clothing and the fog blew constantly towards her, coming in waves that would have made it difficult for a human. For a vampire it was only a minor irritation.

Her vision was perfect, but the weather didn't help her hair. Damp strands stuck to her face. Her face turned up at the moon, full and hung low in the sky, just over Cabot Tower. Another gift of vampire sight, even heavy fog could not obscure its green glow from her sight. Signal Hill was one of those places that tourists often came to visit, because the view on a clear day was exceptional; St. John's harbor to the right, the ocean, trees and small cliffs to the left. It showed Newfoundland's rugged beauty and was just a nice place to go and watch the waves, and occasionally an iceberg or whales if you got lucky.

She crested the hill and took in the parking lot. A couple of cars where there; concentrating she heard breathing and wet noises, as it was something of a tradition that people still came up here to have sex. She shook her head—the smell of blood and the pounding of heartbeats was starting to affect her.

She would feed, but not now. First she needed to get in position. Up here was too public and exposed, even with this small crowd. She advanced towards the steps that led downwards towards the harbor and eventually the Battery. She followed the trail past the steps and out of view from the parking lot. Once certain she was out of sight she made a dash forward and jumped.

The quick rush of air as it rippled her clothes and hair was exhilarating and worth what would soon follow. In the air with her hands outstretched she fell a good two-hundred feet before her hands and feet painfully hit rocks below, tearing her fingers and crunching her feet in her sneakers. A human would end up in hospital from such a fall, or perhaps even dead. As a vampire though, Cassandra gritted her teeth and just stood up. Her hands quickly healed and she shook off the pain in her feet.

She let the wind whip through her hair and readjusted the sword on her back. It was usually windy out here, exposed to the elements as it was and high up. Signal Hill was full of cliffs as it was almost the most eastern point in Newfoundland a stone's throw from the Atlantic Ocean. As with most of Newfoundland, the coast line was covered in cliffs and rock outcroppings, a remnant from millions of years ago when the island was part of Europe or Africa. The wind was cold as it blew strands of hair into her face, but that mattered nothing to her. She wiped the blood from her hands on a nearby small, windblown stunted tree. She closed her eyes and concentrated. Whoever this other vampire was didn't rush to get here, which didn't give her any answers but it gave her some time.

She walked over to a rock where she could sit against it and see the ocean. It was timeless, like herself. She felt a twinge of sadness and thought once more how Joseph would enjoy this, how she would like to have him with her, but she quickly pushed the notion aside. She was alone in the world once more and would have to be content with that for now.

***

Anne was starting to understand why Catherine liked this place. Newfoundland certainly wasn't crowded and while the weather stunk, the people's friendliness and warmth impressed her.

Stopping at the corner of Water Street and Prescott Street, she closed her eyes and concentrated. She felt the presence of the other vampire, near perhaps only a little over a mile away. She turned her head to the left, her eyes moving along St. John's harbor and with the use of her vampire sight to negate the fog, soon spied a building on top of a hill.

Ahh, a place away from prying eyes and near the water, she contemplated. *You are something of a romantic and yet fearful I mean you harm. I will find you Catherine, soon.*

She continued to walk and soon downtown faded as she headed up Hill O' Chips and back into the city proper. Old and colorful houses and a café on her right made her smile. A colorful poster on a telephone poll said, *George Street Mardi Gras, Saturday October 26, $10,000 in cash prizes!*

Why would Mardi Gras be happening here around Halloween? Pulling out her phone she checked on it—apparently it was a costume and drinking festival that happened on George Street every around every Halloween. The idea of going as a vampire, perhaps even Lucy from *Dracula,* would be fun.

Anne continued to walk, using her phone to confirm her reservation at the Marriot, a hotel she just walked by earlier tonight on Duckworth Street. She also called her manservant James.

"Bring my bike to the hotel. It's near George Street." With that taken care of she found herself at a crossroads with Signal Hill and an arrow pointing left, and Battery Road and arrow pointing right. Closing her eyes for a split second she felt the other and knew which way would be quicker. Turning right, she went down Battery Road and towards the Battery itself.

* * *

Anne went up one street and down another, edging toward the furthest extent of the Battery and closer to the other of her kind. The roads became narrow and houses became packed in tight. It was charming and unique, the way the doors and front steps fell directly on the road and that while a car could use it, really this was more of a paved walking trail.

A faded wooded sign read, *never confuse education with intelligence.* She nodded to herself. She had never bothered with education. The world and time taught her everything she needed to know on human matters, but on vampire ones she was perhaps out of touch, hence this meeting with another of her kind.

Continuing, she saw end of the road. She hesitated by a brightly colored red fishing stage on her right. It read *Pearcey Fishing Stage and Twine Store* and was locked with a padlock. She glanced in the window and saw a wide range of antiques and old fishing equipment covering almost every square inch of wall and ceiling. She enjoyed older buildings and objects; a connection to her past was a comfort at times.

She checked her cell phone. *Bike is at the hotel.* She smiled and tucked her phone back in her pocket.

Further along the road, a patio had a sign that read Public Trail Entrance. She grinned. "How unique." The houses and buildings here clung so tight to the rocks that the public had to walk across a patio to get to a walking trail.

Adjusting her sword and checking to make sure no one spotted her, she set off at a fast pace. The slippery rocks and cliffs reminded her of home and the memories both mental and physical came back to her quickly. As she started along the trail, the anticipation built in her mind. Only a few more minutes and she would find her, Catherine of Newfoundland.

A leap over a crack in the hillside that went down straight to the ocean only caused her to slip for a second. The cliffs almost in front of her now.

"Patience, sweet thing. I'll be there smartly."

* * *

Cassandra could sense the other vampire approaching. She stood, turned, and drew her sword all in one motion. Her long red hair whipped about her head in the autumn wind and the fog swirled about her feet and legs where she stood defiant and ready.

About a hundred feet away appeared another woman, the other vampire she had waited for. She also had red hair, though hers was straight and currently pinned up. The red-haired woman looked in her direction, nodded, and smiled. It was a thin smile. *Forced*, Cassandra thought, *and I'm not buying it.*

"Catherine," the other woman called out. "I am Anne Bonny. I created John Snow and we need to have a wee bit of a chat." Anne bowed, not taking her eyes from Cassandra.

The mention of John's name stirred up terrible memories of over a century of torment, and she gritted her teeth. *If she created John, I owe her some payback.* Joseph had left her, the Council was after her, and now this bitch wanted to bring up John Snow? She'd be damned if she'd just sit down and chat with a vampire she didn't know. Her face twitched, the anger she felt rising in her almost exploding.

"Put your sword down and come forward and we may parlay," Cassandra called back, "but do not test me, Anne. I'm in no mood. Call me Cassandra. I have gone by it now for fifteen years. If you knew me you would have known that."

Cassandra reached behind her and gently laid her gun on the ground by her feet. She felt certain Anne was unaware of the deception.

Anne frowned. "Such violence, such hostility, lass. You should have more respect for your elder!" She began to leap from side to side with blinding speed.

I could have used Joseph right now, but it's too late. Cassandra put her sword underneath her, rolled to the side, picked up the gun, and tried to fire at Anne all in one motion. Anne made a quick flick of her wrist and a small round rock flew at Cassandra and struck her painfully on the hand, causing her to drop the gun. Cassandra had no time to draw her daggers and shifted once more, parrying a thrust from Anne's strange rapier.

Before Cassandra could recover, Anne flipped in the air, landed behind her, grabbed another rock, and spun forward once more. Cassandra managed to retrieve a dagger and fling it toward the moving target. Anne easily knocked the weapon aside with the bottom part of her blade and closed the distance once more. This time, rather than thrusting, Anne ducked Cassandra's overhead slashing motion and managed to hook her sword with the curved ends of her own near the hilt.

She disarmed Cassandra and slammed the rock in her other hand into the side of her face. Blood poured out of Cassandra's cheek, but she was not willing to admit defeat. She attempted to stop Anne by slamming her elbow into her chest. Anne, however, once more anticipated the move and quickly turned to the side. She trapped Cassandra's foot with her own and slammed the hilt of her sword into her back. The force propelled Cassandra toward the edge of the cliff, and she scrambled to find a handhold to keep herself from falling to the shore below.

"Mercy, Anne." She held up her healing but still throbbing hand. "I am bested."

Anne retrieved Cassandra's sword, gave it a few swings, letting her opponent suffer and slip just for a second. Then she dropped both weapons and held out a hand to pull her up.

"Mercy is yours" replied Anne and pulled her up. "Fortunately, I am not here to kill you, only to talk. Perhaps now with that settled we can discuss matters like ladies."

Cassandra wiped some of blood from her mouth.

"Ms. Bonny, I am grateful and ready to discuss anything you may like. But I hope you will acknowledge that John was a miserable piece of shit and the fact that you made him a piss off." She sheathed her sword but kept her hand resting on the hilt.

Anne put away her own weapon and moved beside her. "Please call me Anne, lass. I never liked the term Ms. John was perhaps my greatest feckin' mistake. But come, you're hurt and the weather is certainly not conducive to chatting. Let's return to my hotel room; you'll find my tale

The Newfoundland Vampire   Charles O'Keefe

and hospitably fitting. I am Irish, my dear, and it's high time we both had a taste of some fine whiskey.

Chapter 4: Roxanne

Joseph arrived home late Monday night. Class was over and he had a belly full of moose blood. He took care of the cats and let Ginger out. He wasn't the slightest bit tired and did some school work; it was always good to be ahead of the game.

Just then he felt a twinge in his mind and his stomach. It was a familiar sensation and he knew Cassandra was in some kind of trouble. He instinctively reached for his coat but then stopped. She hadn't reached out to him,

I guess somehow I thought she always would. He felt her nervousness, sense of danger, and for the briefest of moments, even a fear of death but then it passed. Whatever she was doing, she didn't want or need his help. Oddly, he felt a little hurt but she had the right to face her own problems.

Be careful, he sent. *Remember I'll be there if you need me.*

In a few seconds the response came back. *Another of our kind is here, but I'm fine, dear one. Enjoy your evening. And thank you, you'll always be my beloved.*

"Another vampire?" Joseph mused. "I wonder what brought it here."

* * *

Joseph woke up and turned his face to the window. The setting sun was dark red and he closed his eyes. Loneliness tugged at him. Last night Cassandra had been so close, he could sense her presence, but he couldn't go back to her. His principles meant more to him now than ever. He had to resist the temptation to use his powers for wrong, to allow another human death. Three so far between himself

32

and Cassandra, three people who didn't deserve to die but had.

He couldn't dwell on it too much; he had to move on. As if knowing he needed a distraction, Jude jumped up on his bed, purring and rubbing his head against Joseph's. He petted him and rubbed his head and found the attention did cheer him up a little. He got out of bed and took care of Jude and Ginger, separating them once more before they got into a vicious fight. It would take time for them to get along.

His parents came back Thursday night, but for tonight he had no classes and no plans. A big advantage of vampire physiology was that he could remain alert all night. Last night he had used that time to get all his assignments done for the semester and his readings for the next week or two. He remembered that Bitters movie night was on Tuesday and with money he had left from gambling on the cruise, he could have a few drinks and make a night of it—and never worrying about drunk driving was certainly a plus.

Getting in the car he plugged in his iPod as usual. He wanted something to lighten his mood so he chose the Pet Shop Boys playlist. He had to tune out the hum of the engine and the constant crunching and scraping of the tires on the pavement to focus on the music. The song was fitting if not ironic.

I'll do what you want me to do
You're a vampire, I'm a vampire, too

He smiled to himself. "If only you fellas knew. Not in the mood though." He hit the skip button as the light turned green at the bottom of Cherry Lane and turned toward the highway to St. John's with the window down. The distant smell of the ocean and the muskiness of the trees all wafted into his nose.

The next song came on and he listened again.

I don't know why, I don't know how
I thought I loved you, but I'm not sure now

Again he found her, Cassandra. He couldn't get her out of his head. Everything reminded him of her. He knew it was natural, they had done so much, and he had loved her—or at least he'd thought so.

He needed a break, something lighter. Taking the turnoff towards the Outer Ring Road and Memorial University, he turned on the radio, something modern for a change of pace. Tomorrow was Halloween and he would need to get some candy but for now there was sweet beer and he sure as hell wanted a drink.

* * *

He settled onto the couch and started to work on his first glass of Newcastle Brown Ale, something he hadn't had in a while. After his beer was half gone the movie started. *A Fish Called Wanda*, a movie he enjoyed when he first saw it years ago, was on first.

His second beer went down well enough. The movie was about 45 minutes in and he was just about order his third beer when a thought occurred to him. *This is how it all started, this is where I met Cassandra and my human life ended. It was two months ago but it feels like yesterday. Now I feel stuck.*

Instantly shaking off the intoxication from the two pints, he went up to the bar and paid the tab. He couldn't plod on as if nothing had changed, because everything was different.

I'm a vampire, Goddamn it! He could do anything he wanted. He was lonely, horny, and he wanted female companionship. He was sick of feeling shy and awkward around women. It was time someone else was on the receiving end of a seductive vampire.

The Newfoundland Vampire   Charles O'Keefe

* * *

Joseph pulled into the parking lot of Churchill Square, a mini-mall area that had stores arranged on three sides forming an open square. Aside from a few restaurants, a bank and a drug store, it had the pub he meant to go to, Big Ben's, and a hair salon. He scratched his head and looked at a big head of puffy hair in the rear view mirror. Three months since he'd had a haircut. It was time for one.

If he was going to move on and try to find someone new, he would have to spiff himself up a little. As Cassandra said, even vampires need to get their hair done. He went into The Hair Institute for a trim. Luckily they stayed open late most nights and he was one of the last customers.

This goal accomplished he went to the drug store nearby and got some mints. It couldn't hurt. Ready as he could be, he moved the car closer to the bar, checked that his sword was in the trunk, locked the car and went in. He was determined to try. He quickly felt his pulse, to make sure it was there and that he was breathing. It was important he appeared human in every respect.

He smiled as he walked in, quickly spotting Roxanne serving at the bar. She was the same as he remembered, a little shorter than him with long dark blonde curly hair, piercings in both nostrils, several in each ear and one in each eyebrow. She had green eyes and a slim figure. He remembered Roxanne from a folklore class on body transformation. She had a large tattoo on her back and was friendly to him. She had pulled up her shirt to display the dragon tattoo to him, and the rest of the class, when the professor discussed the topic. He was intrigued and impressed and later got his own tattoo at the end of the semester. It was just eight months ago, and his shyness had stopped him from asking her out. He had come to the bar once, but again didn't have the guts to make a move.

Tonight he was still nervous, but he had an edge. He was going to use his vampire abilities. He would be able to say the right words by skimming the surface of her mind. He walked over to the bar and took a seat near the end. Only about a dozen people in the bar, a few playing pool, a couple more staring into their drinks, several others played with their phones. Just one guy was talking to Roxanne. He was heavyset, in his mid-forties with thinning hair and a substantial beer belly.

"Out for a smoke," the man said to Roxanne. "Be back later." Roxanne nodded, then smiled when she saw Joseph.

"Joseph, right?" She took the empty beer glass and put it in the sink. "Good to see you. I was wondering if you might stop by again. What's up?"

Joseph smiled back. "Oh, not much. I remembered you worked here and thought I'd come and say hello. I'm almost finished at MUN. You?"

He scanned her thoughts and was pleased she liked that he was there. *He's nice. It's a shame he's so shy. I might go out with him if he asked.*

She rinsed out the glass in the sink and hung it upside down above the bar to drip dry. Joseph put his hand in his pocket and brought out some cash. Roxanne glanced down at the bar and then back up at Joseph.

"That's cool. I'll be done next April. I'm not sure what a folklore degree will get me, but we'll see. So what can I get you?"

Tonight I will ask. I just need to wait for the right moment.

"Next April isn't long. I'll be done in December but I'll convocate in May, same as you. I'll have a Rickard's White with a slice of orange please."

"Sure thing, coming right up. Oh, you can start a tab and pay later. I assume you'll be sticking around for a while?" *At least this time he's staying to have a drink. He's so shy and kind of cute.* Roxanne put a glass to the tap, tipped it on the side and filed it. She fished an orange slice from a glass by the sink, put it on the side of the glass and put it in front of Joseph.

Joseph nodded and had a sip of his beer, putting his change on the counter for a tip. "Yeah, I'll stick around. You know, after taking that folklore class on tattoos and piercings I decided to get a tattoo myself. Would you like to see it?"

That's a nice surprise, Roxanne thought, and Joseph smiled once more. He liked to surprise people, especially an attractive woman he was trying to make some progress with tonight.

"Sure as long as it's easy to show." She laughed. "This is a public place!"

He took off his jacket and lay it on the other chair, then pulled up his shirt sleeve. "Oh sure, it's just here on my shoulder." He showed her the Star Trek communicator pin and she smiled politely.

It's cool he got one, but Star Trek? Such a geek! He's a nice enough guy but maybe we're better off as—

Before she could even finish, Joseph spoke up. "You know I'm not just a geek. I do martial arts, I work out, and I like to go on pub crawls. How about we go somewhere when you're off shift, and I can buy you a drink?"

She looked at him speculatively. Ha! That's not what I thought he would say, it's almost as if . . . Nah that's impossible. You know, why not? I am curious to see if he really can loosen up. What the hell!

Roxanne briefly put her hand over Joseph's and smiled warmly. "Stick around and have another drink. I'm off in about an hour. You could buy me that drink then, if you want."

Joseph smiled back. *No more snooping*, he promised himself. The rest he could do himself.

"Sure," he replied. "I'll have another beer when you're ready." He polished off the first one. *This is going to be a fun night and it's just getting started.* The portly man slowly trudged back in. Roxanne waved to him and gave him another beer first, obviously a regular.

He sat right next to Joseph and held up his glass to him. "Cheers, man. Say, I haven't seen you around here before. I'm Phil, just got off work an hour ago. What're you at tonight?"

Roxanne returned at that moment and thoughtfully moved the orange slice from the old beer to a new one. Joseph nodded and turned to Phil. "Hi Phil, nice to meet you. I'm Joseph. Oh, I was watching a movie at another bar but wanted a change of scenery. I knew Roxanne worked here too."

The man leaned in and whispered, "She's a cute one, huh? Best of luck to you, buddy. Just remember I sit here and we're all good."

Joseph nodded and sipped on his beer. *Nice enough guy. Must be like Norm from Cheers, has his spot and always sits there.* The rest of the time Roxanne chatted with Phil and played with her phone. Joseph didn't mind, his time alone with her would come soon.

* * *

The Newfoundland Vampire   Charles O'Keefe

Joseph and Roxanne walked out of the bar and towards his car. Joseph took a second to shrug off any effects of the alcohol in his system.

"I thought we might go downtown for a while?" Roxanne suggested. "I know it's another bar, but I like dancing. Cool with you? Oh also, you okay to drive?"

Joseph nodded. "Sure, sounds like fun. And yeah I'm fine to drive. Since your replacement was late, I haven't had a drink in almost an hour."

He opened the car door for her and she got in. Joseph quickly went around to the other side of the car, opened the door and hopped in. She smiled back at him, and he smoothly pulled out the parking spot and onto the road.

"That's true," Roxanne agreed. "Angela does that sometimes. So what do you do for fun? You mentioned martial arts—what kind is it?"

Joseph went down Allandale road. Stopping briefly at the light he turned on his iPod, went to the Police playlist and pressed play.

Roxanne, you don't have to put on that dress tonight
Walk the streets for money, you don't care if it's wrong or if it's right

"Really, Joseph?" she asked indignantly. "This is what you picked to play?"

Joseph laughed. "Oh come on, I'm teasing. Besides, you have to admit it's a good song."

Roxanne smiled. "You're just lucky I find you cute. Now focus on the road, please."

Joseph did and soon they arrived on Duckworth Street. *Have to be cool.*

"Getting back to what you asked, it's called *Jeet Kune Do*. We do a combination of weapons and unarmed attacks. I also like going to concerts and I play the piano a little."

"That's cool. I guess you're in good shape. Maybe you could show me some moves later?"

Joseph smiled, pleased with how this was going. He parked in front of the Yellow Belly restaurant; it was right next the end of George Street, the place he figured she most likely wanted to go. Parking, he jumped out and opened the door for her. He remembered Cassandra appreciated his gentlemanly ways and he hoped Roxanne would too. She smiled and took his hand as he pulled her to a standing position.

"Thanks, how about we head over to Dusk? I know some of the bouncers there."

"Fine with me. So what about you? What do you like to do when you're off work?"

Joseph turned back for a second to hit the lock button on his key chain. It was a cold, misty and foggy night, same as most in the fall. Roxanne wore a light pink long-sleeved shirt and a short-sleeved shirt over it that was snug to her chest. On the shirt was a logo of The Ramones, the names of each member going around in the circle.

"Well, I've done Shakespeare by the Sea a few times," she replied. "I had fun with the plays, especially Macbeth. I like the bar scene too, at least a few nights a week." Joseph smiled and looked into her eyes. *She's fun,* he decided. *I hope she thinks I am too.*

"Oh yeah, that's cool. I did a course in Shakespeare and I've seen a bunch of those plays. Lady Macbeth is an interesting character."

"Some of the scenes got intense." She smiled as Joseph held the door for her. "Yeah, I did the same course. I actually played Lady Macbeth, the same prof, Peter, directed the play. Come on, let's go inside."

This was one of Joseph's least favorite bars. It was full of underage drinkers, played loud dance music, and was most likely a place to get drugs. The loud music played havoc with his acute senses, so he focused on Roxanne's voice instead of the thump, thump, thump and managed to tune it out. All the heartbeats, all the veins pulsing, the smell of blood and flesh, it was so tempting. He had drunk just last night but places with a lot of people could still be still tough.

He was surprised the bar was so full but when he spotted a few people in costume he remembered Mardi Gras and Halloween, a George street tradition. Instead of beads and topless women it was costumes, cover charges and a lot of drinking.

"Drinks on me," he said close to her ear. "Just order whatever you'd like."

Roxanne was already starting to shake her hips back and forth. She kissed him quickly on the cheek and took the bills from his hand. "Nice one. Be right back with a couple."

Roxanne quickly came back with two green shots, she downed hers in a flash and Joseph did the same. It was some sickly sugar and vodka mix but wasn't bad. Roxanne turned to him, pulled him close and said in his ear, "Dance with me. Just follow my lead."

Joseph certainly wasn't much of dancer but he was flexible and he found with his enhanced reflexes and he could copy Roxanne well enough. The fact that she often rubbed up against him and occasionally pushed against his crotch only made it that more appealing and he was getting hard. He discovered that he loved dancing with a hot woman in a club. It was not something he had done before and the surge of pride and lust helped to distract from all the tasty blood around.

"Follow me." She gently tugged on his ear. "I'll show you where the real fun is around here."

He nodded. She probably meant drugs. *Fuck it,* he thought. Drugs couldn't hurt him anyway. *It will be a time.*

She led him to an alley outside the club, some of sort of forgotten spot for a patio perhaps. Everyone around him was smoking a mixture of cigarettes and marijuana. Roxanne opened a tiny vial and put a white powder on her hand. Covering one nostril with her other hand she sniffed it and then closed her eyes in pleasure.

"Mmm, yeah!"

Joseph had never seen open drug use before. His parents had stressed so much about the dangers and how it was illegal that he couldn't help glancing about for a cop. The fact that he had a friend who was a police officer only made it worse. While the act lowered his opinion of Roxanne, he wasn't about to leave. *This could be a good thing,* he thought, *maybe it's time I took a walk on the wild side. I've already been in an orgy and it's not like drugs can hurt me.* He shrugged his shoulders, *screw it, I'm in for whatever the night brings.*

A guy with a baseball cap turned sideways and passed her a joint. "Want a toke?"

"Yeah, thanks man." She took a draw.

She passed it to Joseph. She raised her eyebrows, questioning him. Joseph was certain this was some kind of test. "Only if you want to, 'k? No press—"

Before she could even finish he took it and sucked in a big mouthful. Vampire or not, he just wasn't used to it and he coughed as smoke filled his lungs. Roxanne and the man both chuckled.

"Let me show you, honey. Just not so fast. Take in a little and let it out slowly."

Joseph nodded and did as she said. He still coughed, but not as much, after a few more tokes the pleasant sensation of an intoxicated haze begin to spread over his mind and body. His nervousness faded away.

"Yeah that's it, just take it easy."

The man smiled and Joseph passed the joint back to him. The next hour or so passed like that, a shot, some dancing, and back to the alley. Roxanne was quite drunk but with the coke in her system still strangely alert, and Joseph was enjoying the sensation of alcohol and dope. He was happy and had that pleasant dizzy sensation that often came to him when drinking.

Roxanne whispered in his ear, "Want to get out here? My place isn't far."

"Love to." Joseph leaned into her neck.

She took his hand and he quickly got their coats, leaving a tip at the coat check as they headed outside. Roxanne laughed and giggled as they stumbled along the street. It was almost midnight and the streets almost empty.

"I'm just off Duckworth Street, right next to the Pi Pizza place," she said. "Did you have fun?"

"Yeah it was good," he said. "You're quite a dancer. I hope I was okay."

She stopped in front of him and got up on her toes to kiss him on the mouth. "Thanks, hon. you did fine. I'm looking forward to getting out of these smoky clothes. You?"

He liked where this was headed. "Oh yeah, I'd like to take a closer look at that tattoo on your back."

They soon arrived at a red door just up from the pizza place. "Try to keep it down okay?" Roxanne put the key in the door. "Dave and Neal may be asleep. Sure, babe, you can look at my tattoo, I've got a few others I'd like to show you as well."

The place was cramped, old and a little dirty. Obviously the landlord didn't keep up on repairs. Joseph didn't care much at the moment. They quickly got in her bedroom and Roxanne pulled off her clothes to reveal her lacy bra and panties. He didn't get a chance to take off any of his own as she sat down in his lap facing away from him saying, "Help me take off this bra, I know you wanted to see my back."

Joseph took this moment to shake off the effects of the drugs and alcohol, he wanted all his senses about him. He fiddled a little with the bra and then unclasped it. She giggled but not in a mean way. Most of the time Cassandra had taken off her own clothes and he still wasn't great with a bra clasp. He ran his hands along her back and sides and admired the tattoo. It was a large golden dragon with red claws that stretched from just beneath her neck running all the way down to just above her tailbone. Her skin was a little sweaty but smooth and warm. She turned around and kissed him, her tongue gently probing inside his mouth and his doing the same to her.

Pulling away slightly, she said, "Work that tongue on me, handsome, and you can check out the other tats around there too."

She laid back on the bed and Joseph knew what she said was true, he found other tattoos. A snake started just before her left breast and ended by her right thigh. Right below her belly button was a sentence written in small cursive script: *Eat out more often.* Joseph laughed at that and pulled off her panties.

Roxanne laid her head back and closed her eyes. "Funny huh? I saw it on *American Dad* and couldn't resist."

She wasn't smooth like Cassandra. He knew not every woman was. He didn't care though and plunged his tongue inside. Roxanne's moans and sighs indicated the feeling was mutual. He had to break away for a second and use his fingers. His fangs had descended and he was so tempted to bite her, to taste her blood. The femoral artery was so close.

The Newfoundland Vampire   Charles O'Keefe

He was thankful her eyes closed at that moment. Taking a deep breath he concentrated and pushed the hunger away. If he bit her she would phone the police and he would have to disappear. It would be a disaster. Regaining his composure, he continued as she put her hand on his head and gently held him there until he could tell by the contractions she'd had a small orgasm.

Opening her eyes, she reached out and pulled off his shirt.

"Mmm, that was good. Put on a condom and come on in, the water's warm." She giggled, and pointed to a box on her nightstand. Joseph retrieved a condom and got his pants and underwear off.

He remembered what Cassandra said, so he fingered her slowly and gently. "Glad you liked it. Umm, do you have lube? I can go on a long time and I don't want to hurt you."

She smiled and pointed once more to the drawer in the stand. "Sure, hon. I hope you're not kidding, this girl doesn't like to be teased."

She also took the moment to check him out, Joseph had more muscles now that he was a vampire and while he wasn't big, he kept himself perfectly smooth and this at least made him look a little bigger.

"Shaved, huh? Maybe I'll have a taste of you later if you're up for it."

Joseph found the lube and put some on the condom and inside her. Sliding inside, he put his hands on her breasts and began to move in and out of her, slowly and carefully. Her small breasts felt firm in his hands and he gently rolled her nipples in between his fingertips. After ten minutes, they changed positions and she got on top of him. He had to concentrate and focus hard not to reveal any redness in his eyes. Her blood, the veins pumping, the warmness enveloping him, it was so intense and he wanted the connection vampires shared but knew he couldn't have it with her. He got behind her and sped up just a little. The condom reduced sensation and he was having a hard time climaxing.

Roxanne's moans had stopped. "You're one hell of a stud but I'm starting to get sore. Lie on my chest and I'll finish you with my hands okay? You can cum on my face if you want. I don't mind as long as you clean it up afterwards."

Joseph nodded. *She'll have her eyes closed and I'll relax a little.* "Sure, that's hot. I don't want to make you sore."

He pulled out and took the condom off, happy there wasn't blood on it. Her face was flushed and her hair caked with sweat. She was so human, so full of tasty blood. He was still hard as a rock and aching for release. Roxanne wrapped a hand around him and cupped him with the other, rubbing and tugging with her right and gently squeezing and massaging with her left. She increased her pace and finally he exploded over her face and hair, she closed her eyes instinctively and Joseph was glad as he couldn't stop his fangs from descending once more and the red glow that he knew entered his eyes. As he'd promised, he reached over and retrieved a box of tissues from the stand. He cleaned her up as best he could and kissed her on the lips. He laid down beside her and she laid on his chest.

"That was excellent." He sighed as she rubbed her hand across his stomach and laid the other one on his chest. "I hope I didn't hurt you."

"I'll be fine." She snuggled closer into his chest. "You have great stamina and know what you're doing. Stick around for breakfast and I'll have you for desert. Good for you?"

Joseph's mind started to wander and he said absently. "Yeah, I'll stick around for that."

The Newfoundland Vampire   Charles O'Keefe

Joseph had to feed though before the morning, so he entered her mind and thought to her, *Deep sleep. You won't notice I left for a while.*

 She immediately fell into a deep sleep and Joseph gently disengaged himself from her. Searching through her pants he found her keys, then got dressed. He had to get out of there quickly, the roommates in their rooms and the blood pumping inside them was becoming almost impossible to resist.

He locked the door and quickly headed off for the police stables up the street. He had enjoyed his evening but no matter how strong a connection he ever had with a human, it would never compare to a vampire. The closeness could only be achieved by blood. Despite the satiation of his desire it had only left him with loneliness.

* * *

Sean pulled into the parking lot of the Newfoundland Credit Union. *Eight o'clock at night and I'm just starting. That's the way it has to be though. No point for me to be here with all the tellers around, they just get in the way.*

He enjoyed the computer support technician job; it was often straight-forward work and the problems had clear answers. *I never have to deal with the public, which is good.* He locked the doors and put on his coat, shivering as a cold blast of wind whipped through the parking lot. As he neared the door he looked up, and over near the right corner of the building he saw a black boot.

His shoulders slumped. *Those teenagers again! How many times do I need to call the cops? There's nothing in my car worth stealing but I can't have them breaking windows or spaying on graffiti.* He put his key in the Credit Union door, turned the lock and pulled, stopping just at the last second, using his foot to hold the door open.

"Just leave it alone okay? The cops came here three times this month, you're going to get ca—"

The words caught in his mouth as the figure stepped from around the corner. He was dressed all in black, his hair was blonde and slicked back under a hat which had a silver rope wrapped around it. He had a red armband on his right arm, with a swastika on a white background.

Sean stood there, hand still on the key, his other hand fell to his side. *What the hell? Why is some guy in a Nazi costume standing out here? What does he want?*

The man bent his head slightly, he tipped his hat to him in acknowledgement. Sean rubbed his eyes. *Maybe it's some nut out in costume getting ready for Halloween, still though a Nazi? It's a weird choice, even for Mardi Gras.* When he looked up the figure was gone.

Sean's heart pounded and he quickly put the key back in the door. Fumbling for a second he nearly dropped the whole ring but managed to get the door open. He jumped inside and closed the door, re-locking it.

That has to be one of the weirdest things I ever saw. Maybe I should lay off the energy drinks for a while. Sean went up the cashier's counter, bent over the counter, reached underneath and hit a large red button. Any kind of place with money had an emergency button, a direct alarm to the police. *Even if they're gone, I'll feel safer knowing they've checked it out and are aware of him.* He pressed the monitor on the first computer. *Lousy teenagers always making trouble. The Nazi uniform, that's a new one. Too bad Joseph wasn't here to see it, he's fascinated with them.*

Chapter 5: A Good Old-fashioned Orgy

Cassandra and Anne walked slowly up the steps of Signal Hill. The fog swirled around their feet and the wind tossed their hair about their faces and behind their backs.

Cassandra didn't trust Anne. She hated how Anne proved to be her superior in combat, but she didn't have much choice but follow to her. *Besides, the only way to improve is to study with a superior opponent. I suppose Anne has the experience and skill to qualify.*

Anne broke the silence. "You know, I hated John too. The greatest mistake I ever made was turning him. When I sensed his death, I was glad."

Cassandra put on a small smile. She had no way to know if Anne was telling the truth but she appreciated the gesture. They crested the top of the hill and Cassandra immediately turned her head towards a limo in the parking lot. She was certain it was for them.

"In lives as long as ours we all make mistakes," Cassandra said slowly. "I made younglings only to have them killed by John. At the time it felt right, but looking back on it I'm not sure. Maybe a part of me knew they could never beat him, maybe I just wanted someone else to suffer, to share the misery." Cassandra pointed to the limo. "You're not much for keeping a low profile."

Anne shook her head and gestured. "After you, my dear, and while generally I agree with you about not drawing attention I thought here, in a place so small, who cares?"

A man stepped out of the car and quickly opened the back door. "I do like luxury from time to time." Cassandra smiled at the driver. "Yes, for a short time, perhaps you're right. No one will care."

The Newfoundland Vampire   Charles O'Keefe

They both sat inside. Anne laid her sword on the floor and Cassandra did the same. Anne pushed a button and as the divider went up she said, "My hotel please, but no rush. Make the drive as smooth as possible."

She didn't wait for a reply. She then took out a handkerchief from her pocket and asked, "May I? You have a little dirt on your face and neck."

Cassandra nodded and stretched her neck back. Anne gently cleaned her skin and kissed her on the cheek. "I do apologize for my behavior," she whispered in Cassandra's ear, "and for creating John in the first place. Perhaps his death stirred up some bad memories that I took out on you. I hope we can move past this."

Cassandra gently pushed Anne's head back and held it in her hands. She looked into Anne's eyes. There was a kindness and softness mixed with the elder vampire's hard demeanor, a vampire's dual nature, caring for others but always wary of danger, finding it hard to trust anyone new. Cassandra could relate.

She returned the kiss on Anne's cheek. "Perhaps, and I do appreciate the apology. As my beloved would say, you're older and wiser than I am. Mayhap you could share some of your wisdom with me."

Anne took her hands down and poured them both a glass of whiskey. "A toast then, to?"

Cassandra took the glass in her hand. "Yes, a toast to redheads. We need to stick together."

Anne laughed lightly and clinked glasses. Her laugh was pleasant and genuine. "Yes indeed. Tell me about your creation. "

Cassandra had a sip. *Damn, it's good whiskey. I have to give her that.*

A pleasant warmth began to spread down her throat and into her chest. "Yes, Joseph, he is…well, perhaps *was* my love and my companion but we parted a few nights ago. He is sweet, kind, sexy, and strong in his convictions and martial skills. He remains so human, though. He is so far not able to accept that humans are lesser beings than we are. We parted because I kept secrets from him, such as when I killed a human murderer."

Anne sipped her own whiskey. "Ahh, a youngling. Aside from John I have never made another. Joseph is young, I'm sure, perhaps only a few months as one of us. In time he may come around, but you know men. They're always much less mature than women." She looked out the window and turned back to Cassandra, her eyes sparkling. "Since it's just us girls here talking, tell me does he keep you satisfied?"

Cassandra laughed and laid her drink to one side. "Anne my dear, perhaps seventy years has passed since I had a nice chat with a woman. Joseph is a kind and generous lover." She traced her finger around the rim of her glass and looked to Anne.

"Oh do go on," Anne encouraged. "I'm not looking for every sordid detail, just a glimpse of your love life."

Cassandra nodded and had a sip of her drink. "He is not the most endowed man I have ever slept with, but as you know, that is not so important. While Joseph is young and was a virgin with me, he is learning." She smothered a giggle.

Anne held up her glass and downed it. "Men often take a long time to learn how to pleasure us. I've only had sex with humans for the past century. Their stamina was pathetic, but at least some tried hard to please me." She laughed as well. "Has he ever done something funny? Between the sheets I mean."

Cassandra downed her drink, grimaced, and held it out. Anne poured a little more in both glasses. "He was so cute one time, I knew he wanted to do something…different, and I was ready to say yes. He was just awkward asking and when the plane shifted he fell on my back."

Anne laughed again, careful not to spill her drink. "That is a good one, men can be oafish at times. When you say different you mean—" Anne pointed with her free hand to her behind.

Cassandra nodded and they both laughed. "Well then, as someone who has done that before I can say welcome to the club. If you relax it can be quite nice, especially with the right person."

Anne laughed again. "With sex men think it's a race or something, I guess. I've had to tell more than one servant to slow down. They almost seem to forget I'm there sometimes! It's a reason I like to be with women as well, they take a much more relaxed approach."

Cassandra slammed back the rest of her drink. Anne refilled the glass half way and laid a hand on her knee.

"He was just beginning to explore his sexuality and surprised me more than once," Cassandra said. "Embracing with him meant a great deal and I miss it. And yes, I have slept with women before. It was also pleasant, much different from a man, as you say."

Anne considered for a moment. "He does sound like an interesting man and a good lover. I assume he is the one who helped you finally defeat John. John sent his final moments to me revealing the strike to his chest, a statue of Peter Pan, and you terribly injured. John's death and two vampires here intrigued me, so I came."

The limo pulled to a stop and Anne downed the rest of her drink, closing her eyes for a second and grinning in pleasure.

Cassandra nodded. *She's obviously not here to kill me. It will be fun to spend the night with another female vampire.*

"Joseph is a geek through and through," she mused. "He has some rather childish hobbies. His innocence and human nature fascinated me and reminded me of my own lost humanity. Perhaps our separation is for the best." She stared at Anne. "I would like him to be unique and strong for as long as he can."

The door was opened for them. Anne stepped out and Cassandra followed. Anne slipped the man a twenty; he turned it over a couple of times in his fingers, perhaps a little surprised it was American currency.

She returned Cassandra's hard stare as they entered the lobby and sauntered towards the elevator. Once the door closed with only the two inside she said, "Joseph is a vampire and an adult. If I want to see him I will. We're beyond notions of marriage, dating and traditional relationships. I hope at your age you can see that. You're his sire and want to protect him, but you must be realistic. You can't hide him from the world and other people."

"Yes, I know that's true, at least part of it. While there may be dalliances, I think you can commit your heart to another, and make any other sex just physical, not deep love. " *And I know it would be a hell of a fight to try and stop you.* "I want you to know that I would die to protect him from harm. He is not just my progeny but my direct descendant as well."

Anne raised an eyebrow and then turned to walk. The elevator door opened and they approached her room. "You're a romantic my dear. I don't think anyone should be with just one person, certainly not with our immortality. There is no reason to deny our desires, or pleasures."

She turned back to face Cassandra. "Direct descendant? So you sought him out in particular, searched for him for years, I'd guess. Creating a vampire from a human you are related to is unheard of. You're a free spirit, much like myself."

She smiled warmly as she opened the door to the penthouse without using a key. She probably rented the whole floor, so there was no need to keep any door locked.

Cassandra smiled and entered the room. "I've never cared much for traditions or rules and I wanted a strong connection, a much more important one that I had ever had with another progeny."

Going over to the table she found another bottle of whiskey and poured herself a drink, slipping out of her jacket and shoes. Anne went over to sit by the window, gazing out over the foggy harbor.

"A geek, you say?" Anne inquired. "I know you don't mean a gruesome circus performer. What does the word mean now?"

Cassandra laughed and took off her socks. She began to rub her foot, putting the delicious whiskey aside for the moment.

"Anne, you need to catch up. A geek is just another term for a nerd, square or bookworm. Those terms a little more familiar?" Anne nodded and Cassandra continued, "Joseph was the first relationship I'd had since John and while our marriage was over after eight years, John tormented me for almost another two-hundred. The last two years of our human marriage I cheated on him with two men and convinced both of them to kill him, or so I thought."

Cassandra put her foot down and had another long drink. Anne had stripped down to her bra and panties. She was quite attractive, with muscular abs and small firm breasts. Her skin was so pale and white it almost glowed. Cassandra preferred men but had had sex with women before—only a few weeks ago, in fact, with the Countess. If this one happened, she hoped it would be more pleasant.

Anne reached for Cassandra's foot. "I thought you might like this. The foot can be a sensual area for many people and even vampires get a little tired on our feet all day. How human women can wear high heels is beyond me."

Cassandra laughed and relaxed a little more. If Anne was trying to seduce her it was working.

Anne rubbed and kneaded her foot and calf. "I understand now about Joseph. That was my other reason for taking this trip. Living on a deserted island has cut me off from the world a little. I wanted you and Joseph to bring me back in. "

Her eyes darted to Cassandra's pants and she raised an eyebrow, questioning. Cassandra nodded and lay back on the bed to make it easier. Anne pulled off Cassandra's pants and laid both feet in her lap. She switched to the other foot and rubbed up and down Cassandra's legs. Cassandra polished off her drink and made no motion for her to stop. Anne's hands felt smooth and cool on her skin, her ministrations gentle at first. She worked on her calves and legs, using strength that could get into the muscles, far beyond what a human was capable of.

"Mmm, that's good," Cassandra moaned with her eyes half closed. Anne stopped for a moment and undid her own bra before moving her hands up further to rub Cassandra's thighs just below her panty line.

"I'm glad. So nice to touch a woman. Skin so smooth and beautiful curves. Men can be so rough and hairy." Anne hesitated before asking, "Speaking of, you're hairless down here. Is that another trend I have missed out on or something Joseph asked you to do?"

Cassandra was ready to embrace and pulled off her shirt, her full breasts barely contained by a purple satin bra. This one unclasped from the front, another little thing she had done for Joseph.

"I watched an adult movie where a woman shaved herself and I was curious. So I made myself smooth and I liked the feel of it so much I kept it that way. Then some forty years later lots of people did it. So no, I did it for myself, but Joseph liked it. He shaved himself when he met me, something he thought I'd like and I do."

She made no move to stop Anne, who grasped her panties, slowly sliding them down Cassandra's thighs, legs, then past her feet.

"While it looks a little childlike, I can see the appeal," Anne said. "Oral sex is easier and more pleasurable, I imagine."

Cassandra knew Anne's intent and gently put her hands on her head, guiding her forward. Anne was perhaps a little out of practice but made up for it with enthusiasm and, of course, vampire stamina. Cassandra soon removed her bra and rubbed her own nipples as she grew closer and closer to climax.

"Bite me!" she cried. "Do it right on the artery!"

Anne stopped for a moment. She easily slid three fingers inside Cassandra and reached up, putting her other hand to Cassandra's mouth. "Let us embrace then as vampires should and let me share with you how I was created."

Cassandra continued to moan and grind her hips onto Anne's hand, the pleasure coming over her in waves.

"Yes, Anne," she moaned. "Just bite me NOW!"

Anne finally did as Cassandra asked, biting hard into the femoral artery. Blood spurted on her face and some gushed onto the bed. Cassandra at the same time let her fangs descend and bit just underneath Anne's thumb. Blood soon covered her lips and chin, and she was transported inside Anne's mind and soul.

* * *

Cassandra woke up to find Anne lying beside her. Her hands gently stroked her face and hair and her eyes gazed into Cassandra's. The younger vampire pulled her in close for a kiss.

"A pirate, an actual pirate?" She laughed softly and let her lips linger over Anne's. "And was that handsome rogue truly Black Bart? You're not just using her name, you are the Anne Bonny and I gather the only female pirate still alive."

"I am the Anne Bonny, accept no substitutes!" Anne's breath was warm against Cassandra's mouth. "My creator was one of the most bloodthirsty pirates ever known."

"Thank you for sharing," Cassandra said, a chuckle escaping her lips from Anne's little joke. She pulled her face back so she could look Anne in the eyes. "I'm sorry your creator deceived you. Perhaps someday I'll share my vampire birth with you, though at the time I found it none too pleasant."

"My pleasure." Anne kissed Cassandra back and ran her hands down to gently squeeze her behind. "It was a long time ago, but as I'm sure you know it still helps to share it with another. While the sex was quite nice, I certainly had no desire to become a vampire. I didn't enjoy the biting back then, but I see now the pleasure it brings us."

Cassandra stroked Anne's back and gently wrapped her hands in her straight red hair; it was thinner than hers, but soft and pleasant.

"Naturally I had no idea vampires existed," Anne continued. "I certainly would have run if I had had the chance. I enjoyed sleeping with Bart for a few months, but once I saw his true nature I had to leave him. That story can wait for another time though."

Cassandra gently pushed Anne onto her back and began to kiss and lick her way down her lithe form. Anne closed her eyes for a moment and Cassandra felt soft fingers push into her hair, Joseph did the same thing and she took it as a compliment. She also liked to have someone touch her hair, she kept it very clean and soft and was proud of it.

"Oh my darling," Anne said patiently. "While I'm sure you would do your best and I would enjoy it, I did learn a thing or two about you from our embrace."

Cassandra had begun to stroke and gently probe inside Anne and she had just stuck her tongue out when she stopped. She lifted her eyebrows and tilted her head, *obviously I don't have enough experience with women for Anne. I must have let that slip through in our embrace.* She lowered her eyes and she removed the fingertip, letting out a sigh.

"Oh don't be silly, my dear." Anne laughed. "I certainly didn't learn anything important. You're quite skilled at keeping your memories locked up. I have simply had more practice than you."

Cassandra moved up on the bed and sucked on her fingers a little to clean them; the taste was pleasant. "I want to show you my gratitude, my pirate lass."

Anne kissed her quickly on the forehead. She got up and retrieved two red silk bathrobes. "Pirate lass, I like that. Cassandra, you're the most beautiful and sexual vampire I have ever seen, but I know what you truly love. It's nothing to be ashamed of. You're fond of women and do enjoy their company from time to time but obviously you prefer men."

Anne wrapped the robe around herself and snatched up her phone from the bed table, quickly putting in a text. Cassandra sensed the sexual part of the evening was done and wrapped the robe loosely about herself. She began to brush her hair. *I do miss having Joseph do this for me.*

"Very well, Anne. I see no point in arguing with you. Would you let me give you a massage, perhaps?"

Anne poured them both a glass of champagne. "Actually, my dear, I have other plans for this evening. I was glad to discover that Newfoundland has a service for those in the know. Those who desire something more than sex, something a little more…red, shall we say."

There was a knock at the door and Cassandra tightened her robe about her chest.

"Room service?" Cassandra questioned.

Anne glided to the door. "The best kind of room service, yes. These men will not only take care of us sexually, but offer their blood freely and discreetly. You're welcome to partake of one or both of my offers; otherwise I'll be one busy bee."

Anne opened the door to reveal three men in Speedos. One was tall, black, and had long dreadlocks. The second was short but still handsome with a ruddy complexion and a stocky build. The third was Nordic, tall, muscled, and had a shock of blonde hair that stood up straight on his head. Cassandra recognized one of them from their evening with the Countess.

She smiled warmly and thought to Anne, *Very thoughtful. My thanks.* Anne smiled and thought back, *you're welcome and enjoy.* The stocky man smiled warmly at Cassandra as she went to him.

"You have recovered, Harold?" she asked.

He nodded. "Yes, Cassandra. That was almost two weeks ago and I'm ready to serve you, in whatever way you would desire."

"Well now," she purred. "I haven't had in a three way with humans for forty years but I'm game. Just don't use all your energy, boys. This girl needs blood to satisfy her."

Anne closed the door as both women dropped their robes and quickly ripped the meager clothing from their male escorts.

The Newfoundland Vampire   Charles O'Keefe

I need to get my mind off Joseph, Cassandra thought, *and this certainly is another pleasant distraction.*

Chapter 6: He Had a Dream

Joseph was learning. He left the police stables on Circular Road satisfied and confident there would be no evidence of his visit. He had drunk from police horses in New Orleans just a few weeks ago. That barn was a little easier to get into, but the one here had not provided much difficulty either. He turned up Bannerman Road to slowly head back to Kings Road and Roxanne's apartment.

To his left he saw the Colonial building, where he had had the first training session with Cassandra. Back then he didn't know it was training. He hadn't even known he was a vampire that night. He had focused on food and sex then. Cassandra had certainly done a good job distracting him from the threat at the time. Thomas had spied on them that night, doing John's dirty work. At least those deaths, John and Thomas, he felt no regrets about. They had attacked them and deserved their fate, and as vampires knew the risks the life entailed.

He did miss training with Cassandra. Who knew what other psycho might show up someday, so he'd have to practice by himself. The idea from the Philosophy class a few nights ago drifted into his head. *Goodness and completeness. Can a human like Roxanne help complete me? Can she help me become the best person possible? What could I strive toward to make myself better? What's the point of anything if I can't share my life with someone?*

All his memories with Cassandra had become so mixed—good and bad, honesty and lies, sex and violence, love and lust, affection and cruelty. It just went on forever. Out of habit, he reached out for her presence and instantly found it. Cassandra was so close, only a few blocks away.

The Newfoundland Vampire   Charles O'Keefe

She must be staying at a hotel for some reason. It would be so easy to just go to her, just to say hello and catch up a bit.

He shook his head to clear it and dismissed the idea. He took in a deep breath. *Sure, it wasn't as good with Roxanne as it was with Cassandra, but that's impossible. Roxanne's human and I'm not. I'm moving forward. Hopefully Roxanne and I can have some kind of relationship…maybe someday I could even…*

He let that thought trail off. While physically he could make another vampire he wasn't sure if he ever should. Vampire life was hard, a hell of a lot different from the countless fantasies he had had during his human years.

Turning down Kings Road he scanned around again. *So quiet tonight.* It was after three a.m. and with all the bars closed almost no one was about. Occasionally a cab went by, but mostly the streets remained empty. Wanting a little distraction he flicked the screen on his iPhone to turn it on. Selecting a radio app, he let it play.

It's three a.m. I must be lonely

Huh. That's a funny coincidence. Three a.m. now and I am a little scared to be alone. He wished he could talk to his friends but they are all most likely asleep. He didn't know if he could put this on them, he'd have to leave out so many details and it of course he could never share what he had become.

Just before he reached Roxanne's apartment an idea came to him. *Vance! I could go on a ride along with him in his police car. I'd get a chance to find out where crooks hang out and maybe even help him stop a crime. I always wanted to be like Bruce Wayne and I don't need Cassandra's help to do it. I know enough, and I'll help the cops for a change.*

The keys jingled in his hand a little as he opened the door and headed back upstairs to Roxanne's apartment. Once more the sounds of heartbeats thumping, blood pulsing through veins and the vague snippets of thoughts from those inside filled his head. There was a new heartbeat from before, this one beat much faster than a human's and he had come to recognize the smell. It was a cat. The animal hissed through the door and growled. A man from inside said, "Huh? What? Esther?"

Joseph remembered that cats didn't like vampires, most of them anyway, and put out his usual calming thoughts. *Everything's okay kitty, I'm just different, settle down.* A few more meows and sounds of movement escaped from inside the room but then quiet. *Cats, an interesting animal, would a dog respond the same way to us? Maybe it's kind of like in the Terminator movie that the humans always kept dogs around to spot the machines.*

Creeping toward the bedroom door, he carefully opened it and slipped inside. He stripped down naked and climbed into bed with Roxanne. Perhaps it was because he was still so young as a vampire, but he felt tired. She stirred and shifted but quickly settled, softly snoring. It took him some time to fall asleep but eventually he drifted off, his hand lying on Roxanne's stomach.

* * *

Hundreds, perhaps thousands, of vampires gathered near the bottom of a mountain ridge. Their red eyes shone in the darkness. At the front of them was a man dressed in golden gleaming armor. His red cloak trimmed with gold gently flapped in the wind, as he drew his golden-hilted gladius and held it before him. All of the vampires held weapons, some had machine guns, others rocket launchers, a few had flamethrowers and still others grenade launchers, steel pipes and the occasional sword or axe. The gladius reflected the moonlight for a split second. The mask had a lion's head around the top and single tear drop on the left cheek.

The Newfoundland Vampire Charles O'Keefe

He spoke with words of ice and menace. "This is the beginning, my servants! Destroy this pathetic Wynberg base and then go forth into Cape Town."

Joseph had the sensation of flying; he was high above the ground but could observe everything perfectly despite the distance. He turned his head to the side and saw another figure made the hairs stand up on his arms and the back of his neck, his whole body shivered for a second. Another man wore a uniform. It was a Nazi uniform and the man wore the same mustache as Hitler had. The iron cross on his left side and the swastika armband came into view when he took off his long black leather coat and handed it to a woman behind him. The face, which was the most disturbing part, had equal characteristics of Hitler and Genghis Khan. He too drew a sword, one Joseph recognized as a scimitar. Finally he saw the Countess, her twin silver rapiers shining in the moonlight. She was dressed in blood red armor, silver greaves, and silver boots that shone in the moonlight.

Making sparks fly from her blades as she crossed them, she reinforced the first speech "Destroy everything! Kill all these pathetic humans! Rip them limb from limb! They will kneel before us or we will use their guts as hats!"

There was a giggle from somewhere in the ranks. Joseph smirked. The Countess was always so melodramatic.

Mostly, though, Joseph was horrified at what he saw, but was unable to control his movement. He made a wide arcing circle as the scene progressed.

A loudspeaker on a pole crackled to life. "This is a military installation, turn back now or we will be forced to—" Before the voice could even finish, a shot rang out and the speaker was blown to pieces. A man held a sniper rifle and pumped his fist in success, smoke still coming from the barrel. Sirens went off and men started to rush out of long brown buildings.

Joseph, however, saw something much more interesting. From the left side of the mountain charging forward came thousands of machines: dogs made of metal that gleamed in the moonlight with red glowing eyes. Leading them was a man Joseph knew and loved, William Shatner. He was riding a massive Clydesdale and held a curved sword in his hand. He wore bronze armor and a helmet that Joseph though he saw in a movie sometime, Roman or Greek.

"For freedom and liberty!" Shatner cried. "'Cry havoc and let slip the dogs of war!'" The animals outpaced the horse as he began to descend. Among the army on this side he recognized Estefan from Cuba and Cassandra. She was dressed in brown military camouflage and held her sword in one hand and a shield in the other.

he Emperor smiled as he descended slowly toward the base. At the military base itself, the human soldiers opened fire with machine guns and a tank. Vampires scattered and some fell as their heads exploded but then the rocket and grenade launchers fired from the enemy's lines. Many soldiers on the ground blown to pieces by the barrage of destruction. Those that remained soon had their throats ripped out as vampires leaped an incredible distance to close the gap on them. Blood flew through the air, covering vampires and humans alike. It coated the ground, the trees, and the buildings nearby.

Vampires brutally slaughtered the human soldiers while fires burned out of control on the base. Alarms went off both inside and outside the base, and sirens wailed in the distance. The vampires had finished their grisly work, all except Commodus who slashed into a dying man's stomach to finish him off. He screamed in triumph and the others joined in.

The Newfoundland Vampire   Charles O'Keefe

One man stopped his feasting on the jugular of a fallen solider. "Your Majesty," he pointed to the metal dogs, "I think we may have a problem."

Commodus and all the vampires turned as thousands of metal dogs descended upon them. Now it was the vampires who had their throats torn open, heads bitten off, staked in the heart, electrocuted or simply stuck in place by some kind of gooey substance. Joseph was suddenly on the ground, Cassandra handed him his sword and helped him hastily don a bullet-proof vest as they ran and leaped to close the gap between the two groups of opposing vampires.

Showers of sparks and the horrible electronic howling echoed through the night as some of the dogs fell or had their heads bashed in and Joseph saw the Count, Countess, and the Emperor fight as a unit, leaving a path of destruction in their wake. Cassandra thought to him, *Keep your head down and go for the lesser vampires, they fight wildly and with no training, they will be no match for you. Be careful, my beloved.*

Joseph's heart was pounding as he tightened his grip on his sword. He sent back, *I will focus on the mindless thugs. You be careful and remember I will always—*

He never got to finish, out of the corner of his eye he saw a bullet streak toward Cassandra's head from a guard tower just ahead.

"Cassandra! NO!"

He leaped forward, trying to hold his sword out in front of him. She turned and tried to duck but the bullet moved too fast. Her dark hypnotic eyes showed fear as a bullet pierced one of them and the back of her head exploded.

* * *

"Cassandra, no! Watch out!"

Joseph woke up in a sweat, breathing hard. At first he was disoriented. He was in a small, dark room. The walls covered in posters and a heavy blue curtain covered virtually the entire window. There was a small, shabby dresser, a metal night stand and a metal rack cluttered with clothes hung up on coat hangers in the back corner.

He lay back down and closed his eyes, trying to steady his breathing. Reflexively he reached out for Cassandra, just to know she was all right. He could sense her presence; it was muted but that was just because of the daylight. Letting out a sigh of relief, he rubbed his temples. His head pounded and he felt so tired. His body told him it was just past noon. His vampire metabolism didn't like to be up in the day, he forced his aching limbs to move. He remembered now—Roxanne from last night.

There was a knock on the door and she entered. "Good morning, sleepy head. Or should I say afternoon." She was wearing a Joan Jett t-shirt, jeans and socks. Her hair was braided and a little damp, like she was just out of the shower. "Did I hear you say Cassandra? Who's she?"

Joseph got up on one elbow, noticing his clothes on the floor, along with an assortment of boxes, papers, a purse and some of Roxanne's underwear. "Oh yeah, she's my ex-girlfriend," he replied. "I just had a bad dream is all, up long?"

"Not long, about an hour." She smiled at him and reached down to pick up his clothes. Sitting on the bed she handed them to him. "I had fun last night; you know how to make me feel good and you're not hard on the eyes. I just don't want to be some kind of rebound girl, okay?"

Joseph started to get dressed—no point in bashfulness now. Roxanne had already seen him naked. Joseph nodded and then hung his head once he pulled his shirt on. *Of course, just when I make the slightest connection to a woman it gets fucked up.*

"Yeah, I get it. I'll put on my clothes and go. I can take a hint."

She kissed the top of his head and tousled his hair. Her clear blue eyes looked at him, kindness easy to spot.

"Oh honey, you don't catch my meaning. We can still fuck. I just don't want to be anyone's girlfriend right now, especially since you're still having dreams about your ex. Let's just keep it causal. You call me when you're horny and maybe I'll say yes. I'll call you sometimes and I know you won't say no."

Joseph smiled. "Well, I've never had a fuck buddy, but I had a great time too. So sure, I'd be happy to give it a try."

"Good! Life doesn't have to be all about labels and commitment. We'll do what feels good and makes us happy." She smiled. "Speaking of, lay back. I wasn't kidding last night. I had breakfast now I want you for desert." She pulled his boxers off and Joseph lay back and closed his eyes.

It certainly helped to ease his headache and she sure knew what she was doing. The sensations of pleasure filled his mind and body as her mouth enveloped him.

* * *

Roxanne wiped her mouth with a tissue from a box under the bed and smiled. "Mmm, not bad. I guess it's true what they say about vegetarians tasting a little sweeter."

He pulled her in for a kiss. "Thanks, Roxanne. That was excellent."

"No problem, man. Neal is home and you're welcome to have some breakfast before you go. I have head off to class, maybe I'll see you over the weekend?"

Joseph finished getting dressed and slipped on his socks and sneakers. "Yeah, sure, I'd like to see a play or something if you want."

Roxanne scribbled her number on a piece of paper and handed it to him. "Okay, hon. I gotta go. Text me sometime and have a good one."

"Will do." Joseph took the paper and put it in his pocket. "The bathroom?"

"First door on the left!" she called out as she hurried down the stairs.

Joseph went into the bathroom, splashed some cold water on his face and ran a little through his hair. Anything to help him deal with the tiredness and the returning headache. An orange cat crossed his path as he left the bathroom. Probably Esther from last night.

He went into the kitchen; it was very small and dated. He found some bread and peanut butter in the cupboard. He wasn't hungry, but he had to keep up appearances with Roxanne, or the roommate might notice and tell her he didn't eat. Plus he never wanted to appear ungrateful; he did have fun last night.

The cat's white belly swung a little back and forth as she walked towards him. She meowed and brushed up against his leg, opening her mouth just slightly to mark him with her saliva. He found a napkin and sat down at the tiny green table. At least the kitchen had a view of Duckworth Street and was a good spot for people watching. The cat jumped up in the seat next to him and meowed again, reaching out to paw at his hand.

"You probably want my food, little nuisance," he said playfully as he rubbed the cat with one hand and methodically ate his food with the other.

There was movement inside a bedroom, the subtle groan and creak of the floor as someone put their weight on it. A man shuffled out from the room in pajama pants and a t-shirt. He was tall, a little taller than Joseph and had brown hair that was a curly and hung just below his eyes.

He extended his hand and Joseph stood. "Hey there. I'm Neal, one of Roxanne's roommates. This is my cat Esther."

"Hi Neal." Joseph returned the handshake. "I'm Joseph. Yeah, I spent the night with Roxanne. She's pretty cool."

Neal moved the cat down and sat next to him. "You're wearing a shirt with a dice on it. Do you like Magic too?"

Another geek like me. "Yeah. I used to play it a few years ago. It was fun, just got too expensive. Why do you ask?"

Neal petted the cat as she took turns weaving her tail around his legs and then Joseph's. "Well, I have some extra decks; if you're not in a big rush do you want to play a quick game? I'm a substitute teacher and I never got a call today."

His head was pounding like a jackhammer. He couldn't focus on any kind of game now. "How about some other time? I need to get going."

Neal's voice fell a little and he got quieter. "Oh, okay, sure, nice to meet you."

Joseph frowned as he left. *Sorry, bud, I'm sure you're a nice guy, I just need to lie down, daylight doesn't agree with me anymore.* He remembered he should pick up candy for tomorrow and phone Vance about the ride along. Joseph punched in the numbers on his phone and Vance picked up.

"Joseph, how's it going?"

"Hi Vance, fine thanks. Do you remember mentioning that anyone who wanted to come on a ride along was welcome?"

"Yeah, I remember."

"Well, could I come along please? I figure it might be fun." It wasn't much of a lie. It could actually be some fun for him if it went well.

"Yeah sure, come along. I'll pick you up at the University Center at nine, how does that sound?"

"Great thanks."

"I'll call if I'm going to be late. See you tonight."

Joseph hung up. He had for the moment forgotten about his tiredness and headache.

* * *

Driving down Duckworth Street, Joseph was in a good mood, despite his pounding headache and aching limbs. He had enjoyed last night and while he never imagined himself as a friend with benefits kind of guy, he had to move past his human hang-ups. Cassandra had had orgies in the 60s for sure, so there was certainly no harm in him just having casual sex with a woman he liked. His phone rang and he scanned for a place to pull over—he didn't want to get a ticket for talking while driving. He pulled in across the street from the courthouse and slid his finger across the screen.

"Hello"

"Hello, Joseph! Just checking in from Florida. How is everything home?"

"Oh, hi, Mom. Everything is fine, I'm just out to get some candy for Halloween tomorrow night. Enjoying your last few days in the sunny south?"

"Yes, it's hot down here and we're ready to come home. Your father did something funny with a fridge, I'll tell you about it when we get back. Tomorrow night is Halloween isn't it? Well, you might have to leave candy out by the door."

Joseph gulped. He normally was happy to have his parents home after their six week fall trip, but this year was going to be hard. Aside from explaining the new cat, he would have to hide his true nature from them. At least it would be nighttime when the flight got in.

"Yes, that'll be fine. What was the flight number?"

"It's Air Canada forty-six eleven. The flight gets in at eleven thirty-five. Please bring the van as we have four suitcases and some smaller bags. How're your courses going?"

Joseph scribbled down the flight number. "Fine. I have class tonight at seven. I'm doing my last three courses. I'll be finished with my degree in a little over a month."

"Well, that will be exciting. We'll have a party for you in the spring when you graduate. I should go, this will be expensive for you. We miss you and love you, see you soon."

"Love you too. See you tomorrow."

"See you then. Bye."

Joseph hung up the phone and let out a sigh. *My life is going to be even more complicated for a while.* He happened to glance across the street and saw a man in front of the courthouse squint at him. He certainly didn't know him and he wasn't sure why anyone would stare. The man had a coffee cup in one hand and a phone in the other.

Joseph shook his head and put the car in drive, heading towards the highway and home.

* * *

Steve was checking his e-mails. One of them said to watch out for a guy with brown hair, glasses and a goatee in his early twenties and on a phone with a skull painted on the back. He stopped in front of courthouse to take a big drink of coffee. Up half the night drinking and having to move some boxes for that fucking brother of his wasn't a good combination. Steve was just about to cross the street when he spotted a guy stopped in a car talking on his phone.

Well, goddammit, if that isn't fucking him! He checked the description on his phone again and looked back up at the guy. The guy in the car had finished on his phone and met his stare. The guy shook his head and the car drove off.

Crossing the street, he opened his contacts, found the one for Green, and called.

"This better be important, Steve," Green snapped. "My fucking hand still hurts like a bitch."

"Hey man, I got some good news! Remember that turd who beat you up a few months ago?"

"How could I fucking forget! Get to it, dickwad!"

Steve forgot the insult with his excitement. "Well I just saw him down here in a car on Duckworth Street!"

"That is good news! Did you get his license plate?"

"Oh, well no, I only had a second to see him. It was pretty lucky I saw him at all. I know what kind of car he drives though."

"Fuck, no plate! You need to clean the shit out of your eyes. Well, it's a start. Keep an eye out for his car, maybe he's friends with someone nearby. Hey man, thanks, but next time get a fucking plate number! We need to get this asshole!"

"Oh, no problem, and—" *Click* and silence filled his ear. Green had hung up on him.

Steve swore and started walking up the hill. "If it wasn't for him getting me a good deal on whores…"

* * *

Sean pulled into Sobeys parking lot. He frowned as he looked at the towel tucked around the passenger side door.

The Newfoundland Vampire   Charles O'Keefe

Every time it rains hard the damn thing leaks! Getting an older convertible in Newfoundland was not my best idea. We don't have the weather for it.

He trudged through the parking lot. It was pouring rain but he didn't rush. *I'm done with work for tonight, so it doesn't matter.* There was a noise, a tiny clang sound that made him look back towards his car. Out of the corner of his eye he saw it, the glint of light off of steel. Through the pouring rain it was hard to be certain, but in front of his car two people stood, they both wore long black trench coats. Both wore hats, one had long blonde hair, just contained by her hat. The man looked familiar and he saw what the light was glinting off of. *A sword! He had a goddamn sword!* He had the weapon in hand, held close to the car.

The man looked up at him and for a split second he saw it, he looked to the woman and she pointed at him and smiled. *Jesus Christ! It's the same nut who was at the credit union parking lot last night and he's got a friend. I'm getting security—there must be someone in here.* The adrenaline flooded his veins and he ran into the supermarket, his feet getting drenched in the deep puddles near the door.

She scanned around the supermarket for someone in charge he couldn't help it, he looked back. All gone—no man, no woman, no sword. *What the hell is going on?* He scratched at his beard; water continued to drip off him onto the floor. His heart was pounding again and he realized he was panting, out of breath and sweating. Finding a seat at the cafeteria area he sat down and took out his phone, trying to catch his breath.

They are gone again, so no point finding security here. I'll text Vance; if he responds I'll call him. I just won't go to work again until he can follow me. First though I'll e-mail Joseph, he'll never believe someone dressed as a Nazi followed me around, plus he's the only guy I know wacky enough to own a sword.

Chapter 7: The Body and the Blood

Ramin Haiti pulled his coat up around his neck. The cold didn't bother him but he had to appear human. It was, after all, much colder than his native Nuka Hiva in French Polynesia. It was Halloween in Rochester, New York, and while it hadn't snowed yet, it certainly felt like it could any day now.

Ramin stopped at the entrance to Tilt, a club known for great Halloween parties. Under his coat, he was dressed in a grass skirt, shorts and shoes. He wore traditional Tahitian garb that would fit in well at the party. He was happy with his appearance; tall, muscular, tanned and exotic. He chuckled to himself. For the past few years he had gone by Ramin, and he enjoyed his latest persona. *That tourist a few years back, he was so tasty and avoiding the authorities, a non-issue.* Getting the local tribe to pick up cannibalism had entertained him, but he missed the world at large. He had missed the challenge of the hunt, and while he could use his powers, he preferred to rely purely on instinct and skill.

He paid the cover charge and entered the red brick building. He glanced at his watch. It was only nine p.m. and the costume party was in full swing. Some men dressed as babies and Tarzans, and several women wearing almost no clothing. One was supposed to be Britney Spears while another was obviously Jane to go with Tarzan. The contest was $1000 for first prize and $500 for second. *The fact that some of these morons probably spent more than that on their costume doesn't bother them.* He chuckled to himself. *This should be an easy night. It will take a few hours but I just need to get one of these delectable ladies good and liquored up and then take her home for a feast.*

* * *

By midnight he was well on his way with Wendy. She was dressed as some kind of Jedi knight from Star Wars. Her own character, she had said. He had never cared for any of the geeky crap but he could tell she was horny and it would only maybe take another hour or two to get her back to his place. She had moved closer to him as the night had gone on, her body swaying and gyrating to every beat of the loud music. He wasn't a bad dancer himself and while he didn't know all the latest moves, he could get by. He wasn't without charm and confidence, after all, he had lived as Ted Bundy for a time. The years sped by in a blur. One-hundred-thirty years since the killing had started, but sometimes it felt like yesterday.

He finally managed to get Wendy out of the club and into his car. She threw up on his shoes and in the car but he didn't mind. He just laughed along with her.

"S-sorry about that Ra-Ramin. You sure you're okay to drive? You must have had four or five drinks."

He put a steady hand on her knee.

"No problem, babe. I'm used to much stronger drinks than these American beers."

She smiled and fiddled with his radio. "Okay, as long as it's only a few minutes down the road."

He shook off all effects of the alcohol and started his blue Honda Civic. It had several different license plates; he would be certain to put on a different one tomorrow. It was also about time for him to change the color again. He liked to do that every few months. You could never be too careful. His house was on Ward Street and literally five minutes away. She put on the latest by Taylor Swift, not his preferred music, so he tuned it out.

"So," she continued, holding her hand up to her mouth but thankfully keeping her food down, "you say you're a podiatrist. Does that mean you'll give me a nice foot rub?"

He smiled and turned off the ignition as they pulled into his driveway.

"I love feet," he replied. "I'll even suck on them if you like."

She slapped him playfully on the cheek. "Aren't you b-bold? Get me another drink and we'll see. These high heels are rough on a girl's feet, ya know."

He went to her side of the car and opened her door. He helped her into his two story house and took her coat. The house was tastefully decorated, modern art mixed in with some classics, leather furniture and white and blue walls.

"Go ahead and look around, Wendy. I'll just be in the kitchen making you that drink." He held his thumb up to her lip just for a second.

She smiled. "Okay, doctor. You do have a nice place."

You'll never find the hidden staircase to the extra basement though.

Mixing up two Lemon Drop Martinis and slipping some Ketamine into hers took him no time. While he enjoyed getting women to his place and would even pleasure her for a time, he was eager to move on to the main course.

Wendy slumped down into his couch in the living room and reached out for the drink. "Looks good…thanks, hon." She placed her feet up in his lap as she gulped it down.

Ramin sipped on his drink for a few moments. *Five, maybe ten minutes and she'll be out like a light.* What came later was a ritual one that honored any human, made them a part of his eternity. It was better than anything they could hope to achieve in their pathetic lives.

The Newfoundland Vampire   Charles O'Keefe

She took off her stockings and rubbed his crotch a little before he started to rub and knead her feet. She closed her eyes in pleasure as he worked his way up, her eyes opening only for a second, a questioning glance as he approached her inner thigh. As soon as he moved to her other leg her smiled returned.

She saw my degree on the wall and appointment book left out on the dining room table. Humans, so trusting, so easy. Before he had even gotten all the way down to her left foot, her head slumped onto her chest.

He laid aside his drink and began to undress her; her took off her bra and found toucher her perky, large breasts. He frowned, she had implants, saline ones he was certain. *It will make more work for cooking, but that will come later.*

Carrying her to the study, he pushed aside the heavy oak bookcase to reveal a crack in the wall. He pushed the wall to one side to reveal a staircase. Laying her down on the floor he finished stripping her naked and gathered her clothes in a bag; he would drop them off in the Salvation Army clothes hamper in the morning.

Just as he was about to carry her down to his lab/kitchen, his phone rang. Normally he would just ignore it but the caller ID was completely blank and he was curious. Dragging his finger across the screen he answered, "Hello, this is Dr. Haiti."

As he did so, that sensation he hated, dreaded, filled his stomach. Another was near. He had managed to avoid contact with vampires for twenty years now. He had no desire to associate with his own kind and knew several on the Council that would want to harm him. Only the meetings called by the Emperor made him appear. On the screen was a terrifying visage: a man with coal black hair, a prominent scar that went from his eyebrow to his left cheek and the cold blue piercing eyes left no doubt who it could be.

Ramin immediately dropped to his knees and held the phone out in front of him, almost dropping it in surprise. "Your Majesty," he said. "This is quite a surprise. I had not expected to hear from you for at least another few months."

"Herman!" he bellowed. "You have not forgotten what was discussed, I hope? Our forces must gather to subvert and enslave these accursed humans. The time for you to help in this worthy endeavor has arrived."

Herman. No matter how long I live or what I've accomplished, to the Emperor I'll only ever be America's first serial killer, not the artist I have become.

"No, of course not, my esteemed Emperor. I was merely uncertain of what task you would have me perform."

The emperor glanced around the screen. "I see you still like to play doctor," he said. A cackle escaped from his lips, perhaps the closest the Emperor came to laughing. It was hideous even to Ramin and it took all his years of practiced deception to laugh along with the Emperor's joke.

"Finish her later," the emperor commanded, sneering at him. "For now, I have an important task for you. In the months that come you will make thralls, as many as you can manage. I just sent details and instructions to your phone."

"Excuse me Your Majesty, but I have never —"

"Silence!" the emperor bellowed, shaking his head slowly. "You need to focus less on your stomach and more on your abilities! Memorize all of the instructions and begin. The attack on the world will happen next September and we must be ready."

Leaning forward in a bow, Ramin responded smoothly, "Of course, I live to serve and would be delighted."

The Newfoundland Vampire   Charles O'Keefe

"You live only because you serve," the emperor snorted. "Anything less than your best effort will see your head on a platter. Oh, and stay out of New York City. It's time I had a little recreation."

The Emperor smiled and showed his fangs as his image disappeared. Ramin grabbed his appointment book from the other room and furiously scribbled down the message from his phone, he knew it would disappear quickly. As he finished writing the emperor's presence faded from his stomach.

"He must be on a low-flying airplane," Ramin observed out loud. "Most unusual."

Stuffing the paper in his pocket, he brought Wendy down to his lab. He tied her securely to the operating table, knowing that the dose of Ketamine he slipped in her drink was enough to keep her out for a good six hours or more. He went outside, switched over the license plate and sat in his car to examine the notes.

How curious, the Emperor wants me to make these thralls who will return to me and be loyal only to him. He scratched his face absently and continued to read his notes.

"Well, then." Ramin held a lighter to his cigarette. He took in a long drag and blew the smoke through the slightly open window. "I better get a move on tonight."

Finishing his cigarette, he tossed it out the window. *He didn't mention the Count. Perhaps Commodus has finally had enough of his shenanigans. Evil always turns on itself.*

He wanted to head over the border tonight. Niagara Falls wasn't far off and a little telepathy could get him through the border stop easily.

I'll keep the note for a few days, just until I get this thrall thing down pat. If I get more than five-hundred I will make some of my own thralls. It never hurts to have a backup plan.

Ramin smiled. He loved to experiment, and this one involved some Canadian blood. Nothing like a little exotic food to spice up his life.

Chapter 8: A New York Minute

The single engine Skyhawk Cessna was noisy, but Commodus didn't pay it much attention. He had his wingsuit on, with his armor, sword and mask underneath. He had a parachute but had no intention of using it. Central Park had two ponds and he could easily land in one of them. It wasn't like he hadn't practiced. In addition to killing, swordplay and planning world domination, he was fascinated with the idea of flying. As a vampire he had many powers and abilities, but flying was not one of them.

"Sir," the pilot interrupted him, "if you'll open the door you can jump out any time."

Commodus gritted his teeth. He didn't like to be called sir. He was the emperor, but even his powers of mind control could only do so much. This pilot could not be suspicious in any way. *His time will come*, the emperor thought. *All the sniveling meat bags will soon learn who their true leader is.*

"Concern yourself not with me and focus on flying this tin can," Commodus snarled. "You're paid to do that, not talk." He opened the door of the plane, letting the air rush in.

Commodus flashed his red eyes as he leaped from the plane. The pilot exclaimed, "Holy shit! What the fuck was that?" and Commodus was pleased that the plane dipped and turned for a few seconds before it righted.

Commodus was looking forward to this. Halloween was one of the only times during the year that he could dress in his favorite armor and mask and go about a city unmolested and free. It would be a great opportunity to kill some pathetic humans and begin the process of making thralls for the coming battle.

The view was incredible, with New York City spread out before him. The lights, the buildings, Central Park in the middle. He was generally not much of an admirer of anything human society had accomplished but a city full of millions of people from 15,000 feet up was something he could appreciate. The wind whipped about his suit and he began to slowly turn himself towards the park. He had almost three minutes and began to let his mind drift. He didn't have much faith in any military strategy Herman could provide, but Herman would follow orders. He knew Herman held no respect for the Count and was the enemy of his enemy.

Sad that after almost 1600 years, Attila's loyalty has finally come to an end. He tries to fool me but I know. No one knows more about betrayal than I do.

He laughed now as the ground neared. A bird passed by, narrowly avoiding him as he made more turning maneuvers. He took his parachute off his back and let it fall to the ground.

Another thought occurred to him as he soared down through the clouds, perhaps only a minute now from a large pond in Central Park. *The Countess. If Attila is to betray me then she certainly may be apt to do the same.*

He had always liked the Countess. She was ruthless, efficient, and always obeyed orders. It would be a shame to kill her but such was the price of world conquest. That Catherine of Newfoundland he'd seen on the video was feisty and could perhaps serve him in his new world.

The water was now seconds away and he turned his body so he could land feet first. Skipping briefly along the water he soon sank to the bottom, making a large splash in this Central Park pond. If anyone did see Commodus he didn't worry, New York was full of strange sights and the Council would take down any video that got posted. He walked along the bottom of the pond with the suit and his belongings and soon rose on the other side, wet but smiling and triumphant. There was not much left to give him an adrenaline rush after almost 2000 years but this did. He quickly shed his suit, shook the water out of his hair and re-donned his lion mask. He checked to make sure that his sword, daggers, phone, which was in a plastic bag, and projectile knives as secured in place, he set off. The leaves crunched beneath his sandals. Commodus took in his surroundings and reveled in knowing how much death he would soon cause.

A sudden movement startled him and three people jumped out from some bushes behind him. One screamed "Happy Halloween!" Commodus tripped on a root and the three men started to laugh.

Commodus' senses sprang to life and he knew all about them from their thoughts, their scents, and his intuition. Just young people out for harmless fun, but he was not in a generous mood. As they began to walk off Commodus yelled, "Do not turn your backs on me, humans!"

That got their attention. They turned and the one who had yelled before drew a switchblade. "Hey, freak! We're just fucking with you. Leave now or it will get messy." His friends' eyes darted back and forth, moving from one foot to another, their body language showed nervousness.

"Umm, Sorry, man," one of the other ones said. "It was just a joke okay, let's—"

Commodus was smiling now once more. "Oh, it will get messy for you, Steven!"

Drawing his sword in one motion with the other hand he pulled the NRS-2 knife and fired the blade. The second man never got a chance to finish his sentence as the blade hit him in the throat. He gagged and spit blood as he collapsed to the ground. The third man took off at a dead run. Only the first stayed, his feet now frozen in place.

"What the fuck!" He held the knife out in front of him. Commodus continued his movement and charged. He closed the distance in a second and simply used the greater reach his sword gave him to slice Steven's head clean off.

The third man had reached for his phone as he ran and hit 911. Commodus wanted to taste his blood, so he sheathed his sword and made a running leap towards him.

The operator had just said, "911. What is the nature of your emergency?" when Commodus landed on the man's back, knocking the wind out of him and sending the phone off into the bushes. Commodus flipped up his mask; he wanted to terrify the man further.

In the bushes the operator's voice continued, "Hello? Sir? Are you there?" Commodus smiled and showed his fangs, then tore the man's throat open before he could make a sound. Commodus wasn't even hungry but this fool could be his first thrall of the night.

After he imprinted in Jimmy's mind that he was a big game hunter who had to get back to Africa, and to kill as needed along the way, Commodus left the still form hidden from view behind some trees. It would take at least an hour for the man to come back to his senses.

"This way he will serve me and perhaps even kill some friends and family along the way," the emperor sneered. "They deserve it for being related to this imbecile."

The phone had disconnected itself from 911 and Commodus ground it to pieces under his foot. He went through Jimmy's pockets and found nothing but a bit of cash, which he threw into the pond.

"Let him start off as I did, with nothing and help from no one." His mood brightened as he licked his lips and put the mask back down. He was breaking the rules, leaving dead bodies around for the cops to find but he *was* the Council after all. They could clean up his mess.

Hitting a few buttons on his cell phone, he said, "You know the drill. Start in Central Park and keep looking. It will be a messy night. Oh, and one with the red sweater in the bushes will become one of us, leave him be."

The reply came instantly. "Of course, Your Majesty"

Emerging from the park, he immediately saw a statue of a man on horseback atop a tall stone block. The Avenue of the Americas was on his left and the back of the Ritz Carlton was across the street, streams of people walked up and down each street. No one even gave him a second glance.

He breathed in the scent of the city; the air had changed a lot over nearly 400 years. The smell of exhaust fumes was unpleasant but everything else called to him: the smell of blood, food, sweat, leaves, trees and even garbage somehow was still pleasing. The throb of people like a heartbeat filled his mind, over eight million humans here now. He could never hope to kill even a fraction of them tonight.

A select few will shed their lifeblood on my blade, but for now I'll just walk towards Times Square and let the throng engulf me.

Next to him a man stood, not paying him any attention, listening to something through his headphones. With his enhanced senses he caught every word playing in his ears…

> *The leaves were falling around me*
> *The groaning city in the gathering dark*

Opening his eyes and glancing over he saw the man was furiously pushing buttons on the screen, texting, as had become popular with humans for the past few years.

The gathering dark, yes, soon the whole world will groan and grow dark. He smiled to himself under the mask. The man turned to the cross the street and he followed; he headed up the Avenue on the Americas and towards his destination. Cars barely stopped as he crossed the street and he saw chance to make another human suffer. Tearing into his mind, he made him drop his phone and then reach down to get it.

A taxi driver slammed on his brakes, a screech that tore through the night air. Commodus reached the curb but not the human. The hood of the car slammed into his hip and sent him flying forward. People cried out in alarm and one woman yelled, "Watch out!" but it was far too late. Commodus moved in a blur and was there when the man flew up on the sidewalk. He brought his foot down on the broken man's throat and crushed it. He spotted the man's phone further down the street and he snatched it up before it could be run over. While the screen was cracked he could still make out *Don Henley – New York Minute.*

That's not a bad title. The device might be useful, so he pocketed it. People started to move forward and the cabbie rushed out to help the man on the pavement. In the confusion, Commodus simply walked off, whistling to himself.

He soon blended in with other people in costumes who went from bar to bar as they too headed for Times Square. He laughed once more. *That last kill was not so satisfying, but there will be more. Blood will flow through these streets as they did many years ago.*

He recalled how he had helped start the draft riots in July of 1863. What fun he'd had that week! Tonight could never compared to that, but as he walked into a large crowd of people and casually stabbed one man with a knife and slashed at another with his sword, he felt he was off to a good start. Several women began to scream as Commodus quickly scaled the fire escape of the old Times Square Gateway Center and leaped to the roof of a building.

The police, out and about in Manhattan as always, soon came to the scene, with sirens screaming off in the distance but getting closer. Commodus sat on top of the building and focused on voices, listening for anyone mentioning him.

"This guy in a gladiator mask and costume just stabbed the man in front of him and then turned to slice another," a woman told one of the officers. "It was unbelievable, it all happened so fast!"

I am an Emperor, but not a bad description so far, for a primitive human.

The woman went on as the officer scribbled in his notepad. "Then he ran towards the building over there, leaped once to the fire escape and onto the roof. It was like he was some kind of robot or something."

"Miss, how much have you had to drink tonight?" the officer asked sternly. "Leaped onto the fire escape and onto the roof? This isn't the Avengers movie, you know."

That man will dismiss her as a moron, Commodus thought. Wrenching a steel pipe from the roof, he flung it off the roof towards Times Square. Hopefully it would hit someone. Before anyone could even look up, he ran and leaped from Gateway Center and landed on a smaller building. The crowd covered his actions as he headed in the direction of Chelsea Park, continuing to spread death on Halloween night in New York City.

Chapter 9: Ride Along

Joseph walked about the University Center. People sat around in the food court area, some played Magic, others ate and chatted, some people played poker.

Got to love Newfoundland. People gambling in plain view with no fear of police. If I didn't have to go in a few minutes I'd play too, not that any of them would stand a chance. There was money on the table, maybe a hundred dollars.

Joseph continued to walk and eventually went over to a fry shop, getting himself a large cup full of potato goodness. He wasn't hungry, but the smell of warm fries and balsamic vinegar appealed to him and he still loved the taste. Sitting down to eat he listened in to the thoughts around him.

He couldn't resist listening in to thoughts around him. It reminded him of a scene from *Unbreakable*. He imagined himself as a secret superhero just like the Bruce Willis character, searching out someone with a dark secret. At first the thoughts came to jumbled, just a word or phrase. Then, as he concentrated, they got clearer. He could get them not just from right here in the food court, but from downstairs at the breezeway and some from a few people outside. Most of them normal—thoughts about sex, how they needed to catch on schoolwork, how the rent money would be paid this month, Halloween plans—but a couple stood out.

Those dumb fuckers. He could sense a man sitting somewhere in the bar below. *I'm low on cash, have to get in touch with Derrick. Selling dope wasn't so bad, 'spose it might be time to try it again.*

Joseph didn't like this guy but before he could do anything some thoughts from another man at the other end of the food court floated in. *That Jessica! Fucking bitch! Dump me and throw my clothes into the street! I should make her pay, take her crap and throw it outside, maybe slap her around a little. She wouldn't get the cops involved.*

Joseph got up and threw his food away. Whatever enjoyment he had gotten from it was over. He had to act on what he had learned. While the man in the bar had actually committed a crime, this sleaze ball hadn't actually done it yet, and Joseph had to make sure it didn't happen. Walking around, he searched for someone sitting by himself. Soon enough he found a man off by himself staring into his coffee and tapping an unlit cigarette on the table absently. Joseph couldn't beat him up or even intimidate him; it was a public place and Vance would be here any minute. He could, however, do some mental persuasion and hopefully stop any violent act from happening. He went to a nearby vending machine, hoping he would just appear to be unsure of what to buy.

Entering the asshole's mind, Joseph thought to him, *you will never hurt Jessica. She's not worth it. You'll get on a bus and head to Port Aux Basques. There's nothing left for you here in St. John's.*

The man stopped staring into his cup, he closed one eye, his mouth tilted into a half frown, his eyebrows pushed together slightly. Joseph pressed the suggestion more strongly into the man's mind. *You will get your shit together and leave tomorrow. Jessica will slowly leave your daily thoughts.* Joseph felt some resistance from the man's mind; he didn't want to do what Joseph suggested, but Joseph was getting better at compelling people. The man regained focus, got up and hurried past Joseph, consumed with thoughts of leaving the province.

Joseph smiled, happy that he had done something to make the world better. *My quest for goodness may not be so hard after all.* He went outside, and Vance was waiting for him in his patrol car.

"Hi there, Joe," Vance greeted him. "How's everything tonight?"

Joseph opened the door of the car and laid his pack on the floor. "Pretty good thanks, just having a snack before you got there. Scumbags acting up?"

Vance put the car in drive as Joseph put on his seatbelt. "Well, earlier tonight I was at an accident and this nimrod decided to come up over the sidewalk, almost hit a woman and my car and did it while on his cell phone!"

Joseph snickered. "That is real stupid. I guess he got a load of tickets."

"Oh yeah. I wrote him up six different tickets. It took a while. So I'm covering downtown tonight, shouldn't be too busy but you never know. Let me just tell them I picked you up." He picked up the radio and pressed the button. "This is Constable O'Shea, just picked up a ride-along for a few hours of my shift."

A woman's voice came back over the speaker almost instantly. *"Thank you, Vance, don't be too hard on him."*

Joseph snickered. "You must know that woman on dispatch."

"Yeah that's Shelia. She's okay, just joking around."

The radio crackled to life once more. *"There is a disturbance just outside the Cotton Club, man with an axe. Closest available units please respond."*

Vance put the car in drive. "So much for a quiet night. Remember, stay in the car, there will be two or three of us there and we'll be fine, got it?"

Joseph nodded.

"Constable O'Shea here," Vance barked into the radio. "We're approximately five minutes away and on route from Allandale Road."

Vance flicked on the sirens and stepped on the gas. Joseph loved to go fast and he was enjoying the night already. Normally it would have taken Joseph about ten minutes to get from Memorial to Queen Street but Vance did in under five. Tires screeched as they whipped around turns and people pulled off to the side.

"The driving is excellent!" Joseph said. "This must be the most fun part."

Vance didn't take his eyes off the road. "Before the snow comes, yeah, it's a rush."

Vance pulled up in front of the strip club, and Joseph immediately saw another police car with the lights on across the street. An officer had his gun drawn, leveled on a man who held an axe in one hand and was yelling something incoherent. Vance turned to him and said, "Remember stay in the car! This guy looks like a serious wingnut and I wouldn't want you to get hurt, or me fired."

Joseph nodded. "Got it. I agree, he looks whacked out of his head."

Vance got out and the other office nodded to him. "Sir, put the weapon down!" Vance called in a loud, clear voice. He carefully unclasped his holster and slid the gun out. "We don't want to shoot you but we will if we have to."

The man stopped yelling but defiantly held onto the axe, not swinging it, but holding it above his head. Joseph's minded raced. What could he do without one of them spotting him? People had started to gather around, pointing, and some even started to take pictures. Another cop car pulled up and a woman jumped out to keep the crowd back and make them put away cameras.

The moment felt like an elastic band, stretched to the max and Joseph knew that soon it would break. Joseph listened to the thoughts of the other cops. *This miserable fucker! He doesn't drop that axe soon and Vance will have to shoot him. I've never shot someone on the job and I don't want it to be this numnut!*

Joseph focused more and couldn't resist spying on his friend Vance a little. *Goddammit, drop it! You stupid druggie! I don't want to shoot you but one more fraction of an inch toward me and I will blow you away.*

"They're all out to get me!" the axe-wielding man yelled. "Mary won't take me back. I haven't got nothing! Why should I drop it? What have I got to live for?"

Joseph knew he had to affect his drug hazed mind and make him drop it. The sensation was unpleasant, so many strange images and strong emotions but he forced his mind in. *You don't want to die, they will shoot you. There'll be life after jail, drop the axe, do it!*

The man held his axe aloft once more then his eyes dropped and he let the axe drop the ground with a clang. Vance and the other cop ran over to him to handcuff him and some clapping came from the crowd.

Joseph leaned back in his seat and let out a breath. He'd done it! He'd actually stopped a violent crime from happening! At least, he hoped he had helped at least. He needed to make notes. *Searching the internet worked once but this could give me tips I could potentially follow up on for months.*

After a few minutes, Vance got back in the car. "Well, that was intense. That moron probably has no idea how close he came to getting shot."

"Yeah, he must be a few beer short of a six pack. Did I see you pull the trigger once but the gun didn't go off?" Joseph figured the best way to deal with his telepathy was to act completely normal and that meant asking questions he already knew the answer to.

"Joe, I have to tell you that was the closest I've ever come to shooting someone. You've got a good eye for details. Police issue guns do have this extra safety feature, you pull the trigger once and there's a click. It's a chance for the dirt bags to finally give up, but it's dicey. I only had to move my finger a fraction of an inch and the gun would have gone off. Robbie was in the same position tonight, you remember him?"

"Yeah I remember. Well, it's good it was someone you could trust. So Robbie's taking him off to lockup?"

Vance started the car and backed up to head onto George Street. "First he has to take him to the hospital to get the drugs out of his system, then the lockup. Poor bastard, he'll probably be with him all night. So I could use a coffee, how about we go to Tim's on Duckworth?"

Joseph nodded. "I'll treat, seeing as how we're off to a rough start."

Vance shook his head. "Don't worry about it. When I'm in uniform cops get to eat for free at Tim's. So yeah, before you say it, that part's true, cops do hang out at donut shops a lot. "

Joseph and Vance laughed a little at that. Soon they pulled up beside Tim Horton's coffee shop and they both got out. They ordered their food and sat down to eat, and Joseph asked what he had wanted to know since yesterday.

"So what street would you say you go to the most?"

Vance had a sip of his coffee before he replied, "Why do you want to know?"

"Oh I'm doing a course in morality and I told my professor I'd give some real life examples," Joseph lied. Obviously he couldn't give the real reason. "I wouldn't use any names of course."

Vance nodded. "Sure, as long as you keep my name and any others out of it. I get called to lots of places but the one street I go to more than any other would be Field Street." He had the last part as more of whisper, but Joseph caught it.

Joseph drank some of his hot chocolate and nodded. "Okay, thanks. Well, an exciting start so far."

"Yeah, you could say that," Vance agreed between gulps of coffee. The walkie-talkie on Vance's belt crackled to life again. *"All available units please respond to a disturbance at the Sheraton Hotel."*

"Coffee break's over." Vance sighed and stood up. "Must be a full moon tonight, people acting up."

As they exited the restaurant, Joseph looked up. The moon was bright in the sky and full. *Did the full moon really affect people's behavior?* It was an important thing to keep in mind for the future—full moon nights could be busy nights. Vance turned on the lights again and got the car in motion. They sped past Afterwords bookstore, the war memorial statue, and Downtown Comics, quickly making a left turn onto Cavendish Square.

Once again Joseph felt the excitement grow inside of him. He had to admit that at least tonight, a cop's job had excitement.

Vance pulled in on the right side of the hotel by the sidewalk. It was a place where taxi cabs waited for fares and a spot Joseph knew from doing deliveries. There was a man outside arguing with a woman and some of the hotel staff outside as well, nervously shifting from one foot to the other, unsure what to do.

Vance turned to Joseph, "Great! This guy is someone I've dealt with before. He's a handful. Just stay in the car. It'll keep running even without the keys."

Joseph nodded. "Okay, will do." *That's interesting, a car that will stay running without keys in the ignition.*

Vance got out and said, "Bill, I don't care what you're into tonight, but you're coming with me. You need to sleep this off."

Officer fucking O'Shea!" Bill shouted back. "I'm not going anywhere! Back the fuck off!" He grabbed the woman by the shoulders. "You invited me here for the night and I'm staying! I don't care if I'm too drunk! Now give me the goddamn key!"

Joseph's heart started to pound again. He still had no control over his very human reactions to intense situations. Vance wrestled Bill away from Sharon and put one arm behind his back. It was an impressive sight—the guy was at least six two and a good 200 pounds. Vance was a smaller guy, but was fast and well trained.

"Take the lousy shit to jail!" the woman yelled. "I don't wanna see his ugly face!"

Vance slammed the guy down onto the hood of the car and attempted to put him in cuffs.

The cab driver got out of his car and started to yell, "Hey pig! Let Bill go! He didn't do anything wrong!"

"Sir, get back in your car!" Vance called out firmly. "This doesn't have anything to do with you. He's going to jail because she called me, so stay out of this!"

Joseph could sense where this was going. For some reason this cab driver was spoiling for a fight and he was about get one. Bill's face was turned to the other side and Joseph saw once more his friend could use a little help. He focused on the mind of the cab driver and listened in.

I don't want Bill taken in! He's a good customer and I'm behind on my rent. I hate fucking cops anyway and this is a small one. Me and Bill can take him!

"This is your last warning!" Vance said. "I will pepper spray the both of you! Don't take another step!"

Just as he had done a few minutes ago, Joseph started to assert his will. *You're exhausted, way too tired to fight with a cop*, he sent to him. Vance was too busy with Bill and the screaming woman but Joseph was focused on the cabbie, who had stopped moving. Joseph saw he needed to press him harder. *I said relax, drop your arms and give up. Bill is in cuffs and you will lose, the charges on assaulting a cop will ruin your life.*

"What the hell is wrong with him?" the woman called out, pointing at the cab driver. The cab driver had slowed his pace and started to wobble from side to side.

Joseph closed his eyes and concentrated, this was more difficult than making the man drop his axe, because this guy wanted to fight. He pushed more. *You don't want to get pepper sprayed, you'll be puking for an hour. Working all day has taken its toll, you're tired, SLEEP.*

The cabbie took a slow step, then another. He was almost on top of Vance, and Joseph feared that he had failed. He opened his eyes and put his hand on the door handle. He didn't want his friend hurt. The next second the cabbie dropped his hands and then his knees buckled, then slowly he fell to the ground at Vance's feet, less than a foot from him.

Vance had just got his pepper spray out and leaned his shoulder into Bill's back on the car hood, ready to spray in his eyes and then the cabbie's.

"What the hell?" Vance said, looking at man collapsed at his feet. "Well, I better take him along too."

Joseph pumped his fist back in delight and satisfaction. His hand grasped the door handle but he pulled it back, not wanting to ruin chances of another ride along in the future. Vance put a struggling Bill in the back seat and then hauled the sedate cabbie in beside him.

Once they brought them both to the station Vance took him aside for a moment. "Well Joe that will certainly give you something to write about. You don't know what that woman was yelling about do you? I still don't know how the cabbie just stumbled and passed out in front of me."

Joseph lied smoothly "Can't say I know what was going on with the cab driver. Maybe whatever he was on wore off or he finally got some sense. Either way thanks for taking me. There sure is a lot more crime here compared to even ten years ago."

Vance scrunched up his eyes a little. "Yeah, that's true, violent crime at least has certainly increased. I'm glad you never got out of the car and I'd be happy to take you on another ride along sometime."

If only Vance knew the truth.

Vance shook his hand. "Robbie will give you a ride back to the university to get your car. See you Joe."

***

Cassandra entered the A.C. Hunter Library at the Arts and Culture Center. She had wanted a break from Anne. Sure the sex with those men was nice and the blood was tasty, but she didn't want to just indulge in a decadent lifestyle all the time. She wanted some time to contemplate on Joseph and her life and the constant haze of booze, sex and blood didn't lend itself to it.

A poster downtown mentioned a book reading and it would be a nice distraction. It had said *Newfoundland author Rex Keefe will read from his first novel sci-fi novel Robots at 8 p.m.*

Plus she was curious about what Joseph would do when he met Anne. She knew that the meeting would happen and as Joseph spent a lot of time at Memorial University, it could happen there.

*Joseph will have his hands full with Ann*e. *I suppose I'm a little jealous. I've thought of him as mine for weeks now, but that's just not true anymore.* The library was an older place and was quiet as it should be. A small group of people sat on chairs and a man at the podium stood reading, he knew the passage well and only glanced down occasionally. One couple was older, most likely Rex's parents, a blonde haired woman had very short hair and five earrings in one ear. The blonde haired-woman looked off into space. While the other audience member had chin length bright red-hair and wore a Star Wars t-shirt, she gave Rex a small smile.

Cassandra was annoyed as she was a few minutes late and he had already started. As discreetly as possible, she sat down towards the back. Oddly enough, he resembled Joseph a great deal but was older, heavier and with thinning hair. He smiled at her as she sat down and she smiled back. She quickly scanned his thoughts.

I'm glad someone showed up besides my parents, Nicole and Lesley. I don't mind that she's late. He flipped to the last page of his reading,

> *"Your spine glowed red. Is there something I need to know about you?"*

> *"Oh, come now, you didn't know? Why do you think I loved your Battlestar shirt so much? Didn't you notice I look just like Cylon Number Six? Sure you did. Disney wanted to test me out on one of its tech geeks. You got lucky. So, I was good?"*

> *"You're a Cylon? Does that mean we're starting a whole new race?"*

> *"No silly," answered Angela, slapping Steve playfully. "It means the bosses finally granted you a promotion. You'll be featured as the main exhibit at the new Disney theme park. It's quite an honor bestowed upon you. I hope you fully appreciate the confidence Disney has in your work. "*

> *Realizing the full extent of his situation, Steve made a break for the door. Too late. Angela was on him, wielding handcuffs as she slammed him to the floor.*

> *"This is kinky," commented Angela as she slapped on the bracelets.*

Angela dragged Steve by his hair, still naked, to a waiting van outside, where Daffy Duck and Pluto robots drove him away to his new Disney adventure.

Rex concluded with "Thank you," and the small audience clapped briefly.

It was a clever and amusing story. Joseph would certainly have appreciated the geeky references and the humor.

Rex added one more thing, "Thanks for that. I'm selling the book here now for fifteen dollars each or you can take it out at the library." He smiled at Cassandra once more and she nodded at him.

Sorry honey, I'm in no place for another relationship and certainly not one with a human.

She got up and browsed the section of Newfoundland books. One called *Royal Flush* had an amusing cover of a toilet with a crown on the top and another one called *The Dying Days* with a hooded sword-wielding figure standing in an archway also was appealing.

Newfoundland's full of talented people, Cassandra thought. *I hope Joseph finishes his degree and goes on to do something creative, he is that kind of soul.*

She couldn't help but reach out for Joseph's presence, he was so near. Just across campus near the University Center. She didn't intrude on his thoughts but could sense his excitement. She hoped he was having a fun evening and was glad he wasn't sitting at home.

She sighed. This was ridiculous, why was she spending all her time thinking about Joseph? She would take out some books and DVDs, go home, and open a bottle of wine. Maybe some quiet time to herself was what she really needed. She checked out the first season of *The Walking Dead*, along with three Newfoundland books, including

Robots, it also had an interesting cover and the reading was good.

Heading out into the night, her peaceful thoughts broke as her phone rang. Her mood instantly changed when she saw "Countess" as the caller ID.

That goddamn devil woman! She will not leave me alone, but what choice do I have? "Countess, a pleasure I'm sure."

The cold voice on the other end dripped with anger and contempt. "Get to your room immediately. We have something to discuss. I'll phone you back then."

Cassandra knew what disobedience could mean. As the kind man, William Shatner, had said, they had to play along for now. The time would come for a great battle but that time was not now, not yet. Barely noticing anyone else, she quickly entered the code at the door to Hatcher House and leapt up the steps three and four at time; she wanted to get this over with. Thankfully the room was still hers until the middle of December. Reaching her room she dumped the books, DVDs and her coat on the bed and sat in her chair, not the slightest bit out of breath but a little disheveled. Tucking a few loose hairs back in place she closed the door and locked it. The phone instantly went to Skype and the Countesses' image appeared on the screen.

"Alone, I see? Not accompanied by that whining twit Joseph?"

Cassandra stiffened. "He's not a twit, Countess, and no, we're spending some time apart." *He can be whiny, but I'll always stand up for him in front of this monster.*

"Well, it matters not," the Countess snorted. "We'll have plenty for him to do once he's matured a little. For now the task is yours. Book a flight to Paris immediately. I want you to start convincing vampires of our cause. Speak with one of them and then bring three humans to me. I will send you further details soon."

Cassandra had known she would have to do more dirty work for the Council but she wasn't expecting it so soon. She didn't want to help them in such a direct way. The Countess tapped her finger impatiently on the chair, staring at Cassandra.

"Catherine!" she boomed and glasses rattled somewhere on her end. "I will remind you that you do not have a choice in the matter. I don't care about your broken heart, do this or Joseph will be destroyed!" Her eyes glowed red and spit flew from her mouth.

Cassandra knew she meant it. Even if she wanted to throw away her own life she couldn't do it to Joseph, she wanted him to live. She also knew that in the coming battle, she would need him; she'd need all the allies she could get. She gulped and composed herself, turning to her phone's camera.

"The Council's will be done. I'll see you thusly. *A bientôt.*"

The Countess took a sip from a glass filled with dark liquid. "*Jusque-là,*" she replied and the screen went dark. Cassandra let out a long sigh and said aloud, "Be careful my beloved, you won't have me around for a while." *Paris is a great city, I'll make the best of a bad situation.* She quickly bought a flight and began to pack her suitcase.

* * *

"Do you think this Sean guy will contact Joseph?" Marlon sharpened a wooden stake with his dagger as he looked back towards St. John's Harbor. His blonde hair blew about in the wind, tossed about like the ship.

"Of course he will Marlon." Scarlett's tone was none too pleasant. "The Countess tapped his phone for a month remember? He talks with Joseph once a week at least about every little detail of their pathetic lives." Scarlett had her hair firmly back in a ponytail, she practiced her fencing skills on the deck, though only able to advance a few steps before turning about.

"While Joseph has secrets, things he no longer shares I have to agree with you. Some Nazis showing up twice will certainly fascinate this Sean, he'll almost be excited to tell Joseph. What about the cop friend, Vance was it?"

"I wouldn't worry about him." She stabbed at the air viciously, slicing as she bobbed and weaved. "Remember it's not Sean we're after, we just need to anchor this boat within five miles of Joseph, he'll be all alone later tonight." She smiled, the tips of her fangs gleaming in the moonlight.

Beep! Beep!

Marlon slid his finger across the phone. Instantly the image of the Countess appeared. "Cassandra will be on a plane tonight for Paris at eleven. Use your phone to track Joseph's car and strike. Remember, don't kill him! This is just some payback for an earlier slight. He will serve the Council soon enough."

Marlon nodded, "Of course Countess, we have dulled our blades as you requested, and we'll give this Joseph a through ass-kicking. We've practiced fighting together for weeks."

Scarlett came over and looked on, "Do not underestimate him, for someone so young he is skilled in combat. Scarlett, I'll trust you to contact me immediately afterwards. The Council's will be done." The screen went blank before they could answer.

She snapped up the wooden dagger Marlon was working on and tossed it over the side. "Hey!" Marlon pushed her back and reached for it but it already began to float away.

She slapped him hard across the face. "Don't be such a moron! You heard her, we can't kill him. Besides bringing a wooden stake is only asking to get killed yourself. You've watched too much Buffy, lately, dickwad."

He rubbed his cheek. "Well, now that I think about it. Still we have to protect ourselves. I'll keep this silver dagger strapped to my ankle, with my boots he'll never see it."

She rolled her eyes and walked away, "How did I end up on this mission with you Marlon? Fine, just don't fuck anything up. All that matters is the coming war, we need to make sure we're on the winning side."

Marlon nodded, he touched his phone, opening up an app. A red dot beeped on Prince Phillip Drive, above the dot in green letters was "Joseph". "He's going back to his house I imagine, if that's the case we'll have to draw him out. In any case it's around the point of this peninsula, going to take a few hours to get there. Hold onto something Scarlett and please take the anchor up."

She nodded, sheathed her sword and grabbed the anchor and hauled. With vampire strength it was up in seconds, she made a point of getting Marlon wet.

He shook himself off, "You can really be a bitch sometimes you know? Why did I ever sire you?"

She stuck her tongue out at him, "You used to be a lot more fun and I remember why, you paid me well that night but couldn't resist biting, and you just had to taste my blood. I didn't want to be a vampire, I was doing my law degree. You shot my dreams all to hell!"

Marlon put boat in gear and put the throttle down and smiled as she gripped the railing, almost slipping off. He put in his earphones and checked the dot on his phone. Joseph was already heading for Conception Bay, the southern parts towards Bell Island. Just as Scarlett had regained her footing and started to head towards him he turned the wheel hard, slamming her against the deck. He put in his earbuds, opened up the music and hit play on his phone.

> *So now I'm praying for the end of time, to hurry up and arrive, 'cause if I got spend another minute with you I don't think that I can really survive*

Marlon smiled as he watched Scarlett struggle to her feet. *I'll pay for that but it was worth it, maybe Joseph will kill her, I certainly wouldn't shed a tear.*

Part 2:

A pirate laid and choices made

Chapter 10: Pirate's Booty

Joseph felt good for the moment as he sat in Robbie's police car. He had helped Vance twice tonight during the ride along. Though his mood quickly soured as he thought about what he had done, using his abilities to influence people's minds. *What choice do I have? My life with humans is going to be almost nothing but secrets and deception, I'll have to get used to it.*

With Cassandra, he could at least be himself, but that ship had sailed. Still, he felt no harm to reach out and sense her presence. It was there, warm and inviting but tinged with sadness. There was no harm in checking in on her, so he sent, *everything okay? I don't mean to intrude I just couldn't help noticing your mood.*

The respond came instantly, even in his mind she had the sultry, sexy voice that he loved so much. *You're never intruding, we will always have an unbreakable bond. I must leave the province for a time, you need not concern yourself with the details. Just be careful, there is another who is coming to visit you soon. She does not wish you harm but aside from that her intentions remain unclear to me. Remember everything I taught you and stay strong, I shall be with you soon.*

Joseph could sense her getting farther away and rapidly. He figured Cassandra must be already on a plane out of Newfoundland. He sent back, *thank you and you be careful as well, I'll remember.* He reached out and that queasiness came into his stomach, another vampire was close, perhaps waiting for him at Memorial.

The car came to a stop and Robbie said, "There you go Joseph, have a good one."

Joseph faked a smile and replied, "Yeah thanks for the ride, and I hope the rest of your shift goes better."

The Newfoundland Vampire   Charles O'Keefe

Joseph got out and quickly headed over to his car. He had to wait for Robbie to leave the parking lot before he got his sword out of the trunk. Just as he hit the button to open it there was a light scraping, boots on pavement finding their purchase perhaps and his eyes turned towards it. A woman emerged from between two parked cars just a hundred or so feet away. She was shorter than Joseph and her shoulder length straight red hair blew lightly about her face. She was dressed in a white blouse, dark leather jacket and white boots. She held something inside her jacket.

"Joseph I presume?" the stranger said. "Why don't you move your hand away from the trunk, I know it's where your sword is. Perhaps the lovely Cassandra told you of me. I'm Anne Bonny."

Joseph's heart began to pound in his chest and thoughts flashed through his mind. *After everything could it really end like this? Shot dead just trying to get my weapon?* He winced as he had forgotten to lock up his mind. He tried to subtly nudge the trunk open further with his arm.

Anne casually stepped forward, she now brought forth her weapon, some kind of antique green pistol. "You and Cassandra both could use a lesson in manners, as well as combat. I could end you now, I've used this pistol for three hundred years and you would never get your sword out in time."

Joseph glanced about, but after 11pm on a Tuesday no one was around. She would dispose of the body and only Cassandra would even know what happened. Anne held the barrel up to her lips and kissed it. He knew she was too close to miss if she fired.

Joseph's sword was lying in the trunk, still in its sheath. Another precious few seconds he didn't have so he put his hands up. "You probably have wooden balls in there too, just to make sure I was finished. Oh and in case you didn't know, I do have some reason to be wary of others."

Anne held her hand in front of the barrel and pulled the trigger. She winced in pain and then held up the wooden projectile, smoke coming off the barrel in wisps. "Wood, as you correctly surmised, but just one of them. Something of a last resort but, fortunately for you, one I am not going to use." She came over and picked Joseph's sword out of the trunk, unsheathed it and examined the blade.

"This is John's old sword. I was the one who gave it to him, even trained him a little in its use. I am aware, Joseph, that you've had some unpleasant encounters as of late. I felt John's death after all, such is the bond between sire and youngling."

Joseph eyed her and did his best to lock up his thoughts. His eyes took a walk all over her, she appeared to be slim and had freckles on her face and nose. Her hair was a more strawberry red and lighter than Cassandra's. She was certainly attractive and he couldn't help imagining what the rest of her body was like under that coat.

She tilted her head to one side, a smile tugging at her lips, "See something you like lad? You can hide your thoughts but I know what you're thinking anyway. We should get out of here, the musket did make some noise and that cop could come back."

Joseph felt a little embarrassed, he knew it was wrong to size up a woman but he couldn't help it. He nodded and said, "Yeah you're right and sorry, I didn't mean to be rude. Maybe try this again?" He held out his hand, "I'm Joseph O'Reily."

Joseph hit the unlock button and Anne quickly shook his hand and said, "A pleasure, sure we can start again." She opened the passenger side door, handed Joseph back his sword, and got in. He flicked the sword on the back seat and got in, started the car and put it in drive. Anne smiled and said, "It's only fair. Seeing as you're hiding your thoughts we'll have to make conversation. I've met Cassandra and spoke with her at length. I'm curious, for starters, about how the two of you defeated John, she never told me. Oh and Cassandra, mmm, she was tasty and I don't just mean her blood." She licked her lips and smiled at him a little seductively.

Joseph tried to calm himself. He had met other vampires who didn't want to hurt him, Estefan in Cuba and his lifelong idol, William Shatner. Joseph hoped Anne was honest and sharing further details of an event she already knew of would be of no harm.

He quelled these thoughts for now and answered Anne, "Well John tortured Cassandra for a long time. She kept it a secret from me for a while but once this asshole Thomas, his minion I guess, showed up and spied on us and later attacked us, I knew. She trained me as much as we had time for and the fight happened in Bowring Park, it's on Waterford Bridge Road."

Joseph drove down Kenmount Road, taking his time as he hadn't figured out where to go with her yet. Anne searched around his car a little and out the window before focusing back on him. Her eyes met his for a moment, a lovely shade of ocean green, and she looked back at him. They could hold secrets. But she had already said she was over three-hundred years old, so no doubt she had many of those. Joseph's sense of danger had already started to fade. He was such a fan of history that he could not help but be intrigued with everything she's done. She smiled, showing the tips of her fangs, and said "It's good you didn't fight him in the middle of street. John was a crafty fighter and vicious as I recall. Do go on."

Joseph quickly put his eyes back on the road and continued, "Yeah I intentionally brought us to this nearby park and waited. I knew the fight was coming and I didn't want to end up in jail or worse. John was an excellent swordsman and very nimble. He beat the shit out of two of us, shot me in the shoulder, knocked out some of my teeth, stabbed Cassandra repeatedly and cut her up pretty bad. I thought it was over for us but I managed to call in some help, a moose to be precise."

Anne scrunched up her face a little. "That's some kind of big animal?" she inquired.

Joseph turned down onto Topsail Road, taking the long way home to stall for time. "Yeah it's kind of like a caribou but bigger. Thousands of them live here and I'm good at summoning them. Anyway John was too busy focusing on us to check and the moose managed to get right on top of him. The moose impaled him with his antlers and we finished him off."

She smiled, "I saw you stab him in the heart with a stick, now I understand why he couldn't move. A moose, huh, that was clever and certainly unexpected. I've never considered using animals as a weapon, for a less urban environment I see the benefit. So where're you taking me? Obviously we can't discuss this at a coffee shop."

Joseph thought as he moved through Paradise, *yes where? Hmm . . . Topsail Beach was a good spot. There certainly wouldn't be anyone there midnight on a weekday.* "Well how about a beach? It's not far. You can understand I'm not comfortable taking you to my home." *I don't know her motives.*

Anne nodded absently. "That would be fine. I'm willing to share with you a little of my life. The past hundred or so years are rather dull. I found a little spot called Green Island near Hawaii and stayed there with human servants. Wealth has its privileges and I enjoyed the quiet and peace it had afforded me. To be honest I had nearly forgotten about John, he was one of my only regrets. He was charming some 200 years ago and I was lonely, horny and looking for a new companion. I should have probed his mind, discovered what he was like. I haven't made another since and it was his death that brought me out of my solitude. So I have to thank you and Cassandra. John was a miserable piece of shit and I'm glad you got rid of him, I should have done it myself. Oh and you let that one slip dear, I can understand you not trusting me, but remember the training,"

Joseph turned down a small, narrow somewhat steep road. There was a small brown sign that said Topsail Beach. He slowed down so the car made less noise. The road started off as pavement but soon became gravel. They reached a fork and Joseph turned to the left. The road quickly went through a woody area that opened onto Topsail Beach. The car made a crunchy noise as it went over the pebbles. Inside Anne and Joseph bounced a little as they went down the bumpy road. Joseph had the window down a little to smell the fresh air. The smell of salt soon filled his nostrils and he breathed in deeply.

He cursed himself, *Damn I need to do the hiding trick all the time around her! She's a nosey one for sure.* "I'm sorry, I know you don't want to kill me but with the Council and the coming battle it's hard to know who to trust." He pulled into a small dirt parking lot up on a hill and stopped the car.

Anne nodded and continued as Joseph turned the car off, "The Council, now there's something that interests me. I have heard of them, of course, but you have inside knowledge. You have had dealings with them? What is this battle you speak of?"

Joseph was a little surprised. *She must be out of touch with the world. I guess in a way she's lucky, her life is still her own and simple.* Joseph remembered that he still had that chip in his phone. It was in the glove box, so he quickly went outside and laid his phone on one of the nearby picnic tables.

One of Anne's eyebrows arched for a second and she turned to him, "What was that you did with the phone?"

Joseph had let that last thought slip out, intentionally, "Oh my phone is bugged by the Council, I figure if I remove it there would just be questions, so I'm just making sure they don't hear us."

Anne nodded, "Paranoid bunch. Okay then I'll keep that in mind."

Joseph resumed, "A few weeks ago we met the Countess Bathory, I'm sure you're heard of her. She's real and aside from, well a threesome, all of my time with her sucked. She charged us to seek out and kill one of John's other creations, Donald Rathmore. We did kill him, by the way, and not with the help of any animals."

Anne's eyes focused on his, "Yes I have heard of Elisabeth Bathory, I had hoped she had perished hundreds of years ago but sadly no so. Please go on."

Joseph like telling stories and in a weird way he was somewhat proud of what he had done, he had certainly had some exciting times the past few weeks. "Yeah me too. Anyway she's basically on the evil side of the Council and carries out wishes for Count Dracula and the Emperor." Anne's eyes opened wide, Count Dracula was supposed to be fiction after all. She opened her mouth and Joseph help up a finger. "Just let me finish okay? As I've heard, twisted and evil vampires rule one side of the Council while those more like Cassandra, you, myself and amazingly, William Shatner, control the good side."

The Newfoundland Vampire   Charles O'Keefe

Anne had to interject now, "You're serious lad? The actor William Shatner is part of a council that controls the fate of the world? Doesn't that sound ridiculous to you?"

Joseph thought on it for a moment. "It does sound crazy. All I can tell you is that I met him and he knew all about us and warned us about what was to come. A fight between good and evil that I will change the fate of the world. I've chosen my side. You've survived this long, so I'm sure you're an excellent fighter. I'd also say that if they take an interest in me, and I've was only turned six weeks ago, then they will certainly check in on a vampire with your experience."

Anne made an "hmmm" noise and then got out of the car. Joseph was curious as to what she was up to and followed. "You have given me plenty to think about young lad." She glanced over at the phone and thought to him, *I would not have the world descend into chaos. If what you say is true I would have to fight to stop them.*

Joseph found it a curious sensation to have her thoughts in his mind, they didn't have the same warmness and familiarity that Cassandra's did. Also her accent was somehow stronger in his head. Like the years had caused her to lose it a little in her speech but not in her mind.

Out loud she said, "All this talk of your fights and what Cassandra told me about you has me curious. How about we spar? And if in the process you slice open my shirt, well that wouldn't be such a bad thing would it?"

Anne unsheathed her weapon and retrieved a dagger from behind her back. She didn't make threatening motions, simply swished them in the air. Joseph gulped but thought to himself, *I certainly do need the practice and she already had a chance to kill me.*

"Okay Anne let's go, I know John imagined himself some kind of pirate but you are one, I am curious to see how you fight." Joseph quickly retrieved his own sword and moved towards the back of the parking lot. He figured it best not to be near the water in the remote chance a boat could come by. Besides, he didn't want to deal with slippery rocks. That last comment did interest him. Despite his lingering love for Cassandra she had slept with Anne, it was only fair that he was as well. A little good for the goose good for the gander kind of deal.

Anne smiled, "Good, you have gumption and a fighting spirit, I like that in a man. Oh and don't worry, I have plenty of self-control, if I see a chance to take your head I'll just miss. I doubt you can do the same for me."

Joseph didn't like that little dig, it was a challenge and he intended to answer it. He would miss not having Cassandra to fight with him but he had become a better fighter than he was just a few weeks ago, he wanted to know how much better. Joseph flicked the sheath off the cutlass and saluted. Anne crossed her arms, holding the weapons on the outside and made an "x" in the air, returning the salute. They circled around each other, testing. Joseph focused on her intently, studying her movements, trying to remember all this training, becoming aware of his surroundings. He waited for her to make a move.

Anne's patience wore thin with his shifting about. "Cassandra has taught you well, waiting for me to make a mistake, to make the first move. You'll find though, that my moves do not have mistakes!" As quick as a snake she struck with her rapier, slicing upward and spinning to stab at his stomach with her dagger. It forced Joseph to go on the defensive, he blocked the rapier and shifted out of the way of the dagger. He tried to step on her foot and trip her but her feet quickly moved out of range.

She taunted him, "Going for the feet huh laddie? A good move but something your creator tried as well, 'fraid it won't work on me." She whipped back around and this time slashed downward with the dagger and sideways with her rapier. Joseph blocked the dagger rather painfully with his forearm and the sword with his own. Remembering his martial arts, he kicked her in the stomach and sent her back a few feet.

Anne made an "umph" noise and coughed. "Crafty, I see it's time to step up my game."

Anne came at him again this time she flipped in the air and attempted to kick him with both feet, a front kick and then a roundhouse with the left and then slash with both weapons. He wasn't expecting it and her second kick caught him on the side of his head. He stumbled and fell, but managed to hold onto his sword as he rolled to the side. Fortunately, the impact kept him away from the weapons. His vision swam for a split second. Anne ran and leaped in the air. Joseph jumped behind a garbage can at the last second and Anne accidently caught the hilt of her sword in a gap in the metal container. Joseph's head started to pound with a headache and he was pissed. He slashed downward with his free hand in a chopping motion, striking her hand and causing her to lose her grip on her sword. Joseph continued the motion and slashed at the dagger in her hand with his sword, breaking the weapon in two. He then made a wide slash in the front of her puffy shirt, exposing her bra and creating a small gash of blood along her cleavage.

Anne winced in pain but in one swift motion hit him with the remaining hilt of the dagger, delivering a vicious uppercut. She then connected her knee with his groin before he could recover. Joseph doubled over with the pain and dropped his weapon. Anne jumped back to the garbage can and retrieved her sword. Joseph saw her in doubles and triples. No teeth knocked out but if he was human his jaw would be smashed in two; as a vampire it just hurt like hell. He felt his mouth begin to fill with blood and spit out a piece of his tongue he had bitten off. His sword was too far away but he kept his two small wooden daggers in his coat, she wouldn't know about them.

Anne kicked his sword a little further away and approached him. She pointed the sword mere inches from his head it and said in a smug tone, "You fought well enough lad, but it's time now for you to ye…" She never got the last word out. Joseph turned his eyes up and spat a mouthful of blood in her face, she was surprised and closed her eyes instinctually. Joseph pushed her sword away from his head with one dagger and leaped forward. He slammed her in the head with the butt of other dagger and she stumbled. Joseph quickly climbed on top of her chest and pressed one dagger to her throat and the other to her chest right above her heart.

He growled and said in an angry hoarse voice, "I will never yield to anyone ever ag . . ."

Incredibly she smiled and he felt with displeasure her blade start to cut into the base of his neck. He had forgotten to disarm her and now she had him in an iron grip.

She smiled, "Most devious and well fought. You don't have to yield. Unless we both want to die tonight I propose we call it a draw."

Joseph nodded and let his weapons fall to the ground. He turned his head and spat out blood once more, thankfully this time a lot less as his regeneration kicked in. He rolled back onto the ground exhausted, still waiting for his vision to fully clear. Anne kicked at the remains of her dagger and sheathed her sword. She probed the gash on her chest and winced. "Silver weapon. John was certainly not a friendly man. With the ordeals you've had, I see why you use it. Those wooden daggers, I must commend you Joseph, I haven't come that close to losing a fight in well over a hundred years. You fought better than Cassandra did. An impressive feat for someone so young." She threw away her bra in the garbage can, the blood had soaked and ruined it. She had smaller breasts than Cassandra, perky and firm. She was a little smaller than Cassandra, maybe twenty pounds lighter and a good four inches shorter. With her coat off Joseph was fixated on this beautiful sexy, half-naked woman. She peered at him through her eyelashes, not shy or bothering to cover up.

Joseph had to make a decision, despite the pain he was in he was getting aroused. A fight did that to him every time and even though he had drank deeply from the horses just the other night, he wanted to taste her blood. Maybe learn some of her secrets. He even wanted her to taste his. As Cassandra had said, and he had found to be true, sex with a human paled in comparison. Blood was everything now and in it lay the greatest pleasure. Anne took off her shirt, her stomach was flat and smooth, and her belly button protruded outwards and her skin shone in the moonlight.

"Show me what else you're skilled at laddie boy, I'm no lady and one of these picnic tables will do fine," she proposed.

Joseph was fully erect but he had to know, had to be certain if what she said earlier was true. He slowly began to take off his jacket and reached out with his mind. Cassandra was in the air, perhaps flying somewhere over the Atlantic Ocean, but distance didn't matter when a creator was involved. Her felt her warm presence enter his mind, her thoughts filled with concern. *Beloved are you safe? I felt danger and strong anxiety from you a moment ago.*

Joseph saw Anne saunter over to a picnic table, laying her sword and dagger fragments on the ground. She swayed her hips in a striptease, slowly unbuttoning her jeans one button at a time. Joseph also appreciated the sense of safety Cassandra projected and returned to the mental conversation. *Yes I'm okay, I met with Anne as you might have guessed and she wanted to test my fighting skills. We had a rather fierce encounter but I'm fine, just a little sore and bruised. I'm starting to trust her, to be honest.*

Cassandra's thoughts took on the usual peaceful and reassuring tone as she replied, *I knew she would come, I'm certain you handled yourself well. I had a similar meeting with her, she can be trusted to not kill either of us but I'm not certain of much more than that. I suppose I should share with you, I am off to meet the Countess in Paris. She wants me to make others of our kind and I saw no way to refuse her. She said you will receive a visit soon enough, so be prepared.*

Anne pulled off her shoes and let them fall to the ground one by one. She then slowly shimmed out of her jeans. Her legs, shorter than Cassandra's, showed muscles and veins. She lifted her butt into the air for him.

Concentrating on his conversation again he responded, *Thank you for doing it and taking on that burden. I know someday I may make another but I dread doing it for her…for them. I'm afraid I have to ask you something, Anne said you slept with her, is that true?*

Joseph felt a pause and Anne absently took off her socks. She did it in a playful fun way that made him smile. A tinge of sadness and regret came from Cassandra's reply, *yes Joseph it's true. You know I am a very sexual person as you will soon discover sex with a human does little for us, only the blood of our kind brings us true pleasure. I let myself be seduced and I let the reality of our separation sink in and I didn't want to be alone that night. I sense from your thoughts you'll do the same, so you're certainly in no position to judge. No matter what you do with her, I know she will never have the connection we share. Love whom you choose, learn from her and try to experience her memories, it will benefit you in the long run.*

She was right, he had had sex with Roxanne and was about to do the same with Anne. Whatever was still in his heart for Cassandra, right now a sexy vampire pirate stood naked before him and he wanted her. She moved her hand down between her legs and leaned back on the table, she had a little hair down there and was wet and excited to be with him. Joseph quickly took off his shirt, pants and underwear, smiling and moving towards her. He couldn't resist a joke, "Thank you for the show and I have always wanted a little pirate booty."

Anne laughed, it was a light and happy. "You're a cute one, now get over her and bite me. I want to taste your blood and feel you inside me. Later I'll put your mouth to good use but for now claim your prize. I'm a treasure you won't have search for."

Joseph ran over to her and pressed his lips firmly to hers. Blood flowed into his mouth and as he entered her, she bit down hard on his neck. Her nails made a trail of blood up his back as the picnic table creaked beneath them.

Chapter 11: You reap what you sow

Joseph pulled his shirt on, watching absently as Anne got dressed beside him. He could see his breath but as a vampire couldn't feel the cold, or rather it had no effect on him.

"Cassandra has taught you well, that was good."

Joseph came over and wrapped his arms around her stomach, pulling her in for kiss.

"Good but not great? I loved it, you're excellent, see you again soon?"

She reached around and grabbed his butt, squeezing and pulling him tight. She kissed him back and licked his ear, then whispered in it. "Men have such fragile egos, it was the best I've had in over a century. Don't worry, you'll see me again soon."

She gently slipped out of his grasp and pulled her shirt on. "Wait a second, I got from our embrace that you haven't had sex with any male vampire in a hundred years!" He arched his eyebrow and leaned forward on one foot.

Anne laughed. "Oh you got that did you? Joseph! I'm having fun with you, don't take everything so seriously. I'm anxious to explore this place and I'd like to be alone, tomorrow I'll be in the mood for something else." She winked at him as she zipped up her jacket.

Joseph smiled and relaxed. He picked up her rapier and handed it to her. "Yeah I do like the sound of that. You sure I can't give you a lift? It's a long walk to the harbor."

She put her sword under her coat and picked up the dagger hilt, putting it a pocket. "It might take an hour. Remember I can run through the woods and jump from one rooftop to another. Thanks for the offer though."

The Newfoundland Vampire   Charles O'Keefe

He nodded and picked up his own sword, putting it back in the sheath. "Okay, you're welcome, have a good night."

She stepped forward got up her toes, kissing him fiercely. "Something to remember me by, night brown eyes."

He smiled at her, blushing just a little, "Night Anne," only a blur of motion and the rustling of branches told him she was gone.

Joseph laid his sword in the back seat of the car and sat on the picnic table. He breathed in the night air and let out a long breath. *Anne, maybe she's the vampire for me. She certainly is fun and I do love redheads.* He took his phone out of his pocket and flicked his finger across the screen. He opened his e-mail and found one from Sean. It read,

Joseph, I've had the weirdest thing happen to me lately. First a guy showed up at the credit union the other night dressed as a Nazi, then two people in the Sobey's parking lot showed up dressed the same and one of them had a sword. I've already told the cops and Vance knows too. I figure you'd like to follow the case, if they end up in court.

His eyes darted up, there was a sound, no two sounds. The sounds of crunching and scraping of boots on rocks nearby. He reached out with his senses, there was Anne about a half-mile away and just a few-hundred feet away two other vampires. *Jesus Christ dressed as a Nazi! That could be the Count himself. How could I be so stupid? Not checking for others, if the Countess has plans for Cassandra, has her going to France, they must have wanted me alone, maybe she wants to kill us one at a time!*

He ran back to the car and flung the door open, he could hear them coming. He got his sword and jumped to the trunk. Fumbling with the keys he managed to hit the button and get his gun. He looked up at three other sounds, a thump, followed by a whirl, click and the snikt sound he knew all too well as the drawing of a sword. A woman stood on top of a picnic table, a crossbow in hand aimed at him. She had blonde hair, pinned up in the back with a sleek black track suit on, also what looked like a bullet proof vest. Standing beside the table was a man, tall, also with blonde hair. He had a pistol in one hand, with some kind of silencer on the end and pointed it at him. He was also wearing a large duffle bag on his back.

"Joseph I believe? We're here on the behalf of the Countess."

Joseph pointed the gun at the woman. "Leave me alone! I've killed before and I'll do it again. You think you can threaten me and my friend? Go now or you'll regret it!" He locked his thoughts up tight to hide it from these vampires and from Cassandra, she couldn't help him now. *I have to stall and hope.* He sent to his thoughts to Anne, *if you can hear me, please come back. That council I mentioned before sent two vampires here to kill me. I need help, I can't handle them both alone.*

"Why don't we just kill him Marlon? We can tell the Countess he wouldn't listen, make another vamp before we leave. Sean was it? He seemed brave enough and I'm sure he would be tasty." Her eyes glowed red and she licked her lips.

"Joseph, I know what you're thinking. I can hit Scarlett up there right in the head and Marlon isn't close enough to shoot me dead, he's not that good a shot." Marlon squeezed the trigger and a quiet thwack sound came out as the bullet went behind Joseph and dirt sprayed at his feet. He jumped forward, in his panic almost dropping the gun. "Let me tell you boy, you'd be wrong. I could take your nose right off your face from here and Scarlett, she's a dead eye too."

Fuck! I'm even more out in the open. This could be it, I don't . . . I can't, he's right even if I get one the other will kill me, I'll die here and they'll throw my body out in the ocean. His heart pounded in his chest, so hard he thought it would explode, beads of sweat broke out on his forehead. He could hardly hear himself think with the thumping in his ears.

"Fine I give! You lousy son a bitch you got me, you and your partner. Just tell me why, I've done everything the Council wanted, why kill me now?"

Marlon laughed and slapped his leg. Scarlett just grinned and kept the crossbow leveled at him. He put away his pistol in a holster at his hip. "Kill you? Now why would we do that? Don't listen to Scarlett, I know firsthand making a youngling is a lot of work and they don't always turn out the way you'd hope." She never looked away from Joseph but her mouth opened and something like a snarl came out.

Marlon made her and they hate each other, this could benefit me. He checked again and felt something wonderful, Anne was getting closer. *Let's see how they like it with even odds.*

"No we're just hear to teach you a lesson. Seems a while back you and Cassandra bested Elizabeth in combat. She didn't take kindly to that, so we're for payback. Now put that gun and sword in the trunk, or I'll shoot both of your hands."

Marlon said the last part so calmly, it scared him and he obeyed. *The Countess sure knows how to hold a grudge.* He put his sword and pistol in the trunk and walked forward with his hands up. *They don't know about my wooden daggers though,* he smothered a grin.

"There we go! Isn't it much better when we all get along?" He took the duffle bag off his back and unzipped it. He reached inside and took out two swords and a steel rod. Scarlett jumped down and he handed her a sword. She laid the crossbow on the picnic table and took it, her eyes only leaving Joseph's for a split second.

Marlon started to take off his vest. "You both have swords and I have nothing? Not exactly a fair fight."

"Oh these?" Marlon picked up the sword and slide it across his palm, it didn't draw blood.

Joseph drew his eyebrows together and then breathed a sigh of relief. *Dull, huh, they really don't want to kill me but what I am supposed to fight with?* He moved forward, accepting that the fight will at least go on for a minute or so.

"They're dull dumbass, you remind me of Marlon, slow on the uptake. Catch!" Scarlett threw the metal rod at Joseph, he caught in and made a whump sound, staggering back and almost falling on the ground.

Joseph examined the rod, it was heavy and each end had smaller round pieces, as if it could flick out, it was similar to his police baton. He flicked one end hard and it came out, giving it another hard flick it locked in place. He did the same with the other end. He gave it a few twirls and strikes. The final swing hiding it behind his back. *Luckily I've trained with a bo staff, this is heavier and a little awkward but I can manage, at least until Anne shows up.* He checked again, she was close, off in the woods somewhere. *Anne, please keep an eye on me, I've never fought two vampires before.*

Marlon had his sword out, as did Scarlett. They spread about ten feet apart from each other. "How about that? You do have some training with the staff. The real questions is, have you found your balls?"

Joseph bared his fangs, gripping the rod with his right hand tight. With the other he used his fingers to make a come here motion. "Shut your damn mouth and let's get this started! I haven't got all night!" Any soreness he felt from the fight with Anne was gone, he focused only on his opponents and pushed any pain away.

Scarlett let out small giggle. "He does like to talk and I'm getting bored." She advanced as did Marlon. He spit towards Joseph and his eyes flashed red. "I'm going to enjoy this."

Marlon struck high and Scarlett low. Joseph managed to block them both, the rod vibrated in his hands and he grunted with the pain, almost losing his grip. He jumped back and started to twirl the rod end over end, spinning it as fast as he could.

"We can't kill you but she didn't say anything about breaking bones!" Marlon nearly spat the words as he retreated.

Joseph did his best but he couldn't swing at both of them, Scarlett made a quick feint and got behind him, she struck a glancing blow on his hip and he staggered with the pain. Joseph felt it travel in hot waves up his side, *bruised but not broken, yet*. He gritted his teeth and pushed it aside.

"Jesus!" Joseph went down on one knee, hoping he could fool them. The ruse worked, Marlon came in, trying to hit him in the head. Joseph got his rod up and with the other end drilled him in the balls, he heard a satisfying crunch. Joseph had no problem fighting dirty two against one.

Marlon cried out, "Son of a bitch!" He doubled over with the pain, falling to the ground. Joseph smiled and kept moving. Scarlett swiped at his injured side again but Joseph managed to side-step away.

"Not bad twerp, that's the most action Marlon has had in weeks."

Joseph couldn't help but smile a little. *Use your surroundings*, he thought, *and keep them off balance*. He rolled with the rod under him, it hurt but it got him closer to the picnic table and the crossbow. Marlon stood back up and drew a dagger from a sheath on his leg. "You're not the only one who can fight dirty asshole!" He advanced with sword and dagger in hand. Joseph's smiled vanished, *Marlon must have an incredible pain tolerance*.

Joseph dropped his rod and grabbed the crossbow, firing at Scarlett point blank. It had a kick and he missed her head, the bolt stuck in the bottom of her vest, knocking her to the ground, there was no blood.

"Fucking dammit!" Joseph cursed in frustration. Quickly dropping the bow and picking up the rod once more.

"That wasn't nice shithead! I don't like cheaters!" Without missing a beat she jumped in the air and delivered and back kick to his chest, it send him flying over the picnic table and landing on the ground, the rod slipping from his grip.

Marlon leaped in the air and Joseph just managed to roll out of the way in time, the dagger sticking in the ground. Joseph got to his rod but Scarlett was there and slammed the blade onto the right side of ribs, there was a sickening crunch and the pain exploded inside him.

"Argh!" The pain was agonizing and he struck out blindly, shoving the rod into her chest and pushing her back. It was hard to breathe so he shut it off, refusing to give in. He stood and swung the rod in both hands like a bat, hoping that its momentum would catch Marlon, the extra reach saved him and he heard a satisfying crunch as it connected with his face.

There was a strangled cry of pain from Marlon, it came out more like a moan with his broken jaw. *Anne*, Joseph screamed at her mentally, *anytime would be good!* Joseph kept moving, rolling on the ground and pulling grass and dirt in his fingers. Scarlett leapt at him, he propped himself up with the rod in time to block her sword and flung dirt at her eyes, she anticipated, closed her eyes and delivered a swift right kick to his left side, he dropped the rod and fell over with the pain.

Joseph knew Marlon wanted more than pain and broken bones, he meant to kill him or at least cut something off.

Joseph had hurt him, embarrassed him and know it was a matter of pride. Scarlett brought her sword down on his foot and there was another crunch, a guttural growl erupted from Joseph's lips and he forced himself to move, just in time as Marlon's sword swished through air, just missing his head. Luckily for him Scarlett's sword was in the way and he accidently disarmed her.

Joseph looked about desperately, the rod was only a few feet away but he knew his foot wouldn't work, from the corner of his eye he saw Anne approaching, taking aim with her antique pistol. *I need to distract them, just for a moment more, give her a good shot.* Gritting his teeth against the pain he forced himself up on one foot and hopped towards the rod, rolling and grabbing it from the ground. Once more he just managed to block both weapons and swirled to the left to try and sweep Marlon's legs. Marlon anticipated and sliced with his dagger to the right, it cut across Joseph from his left shoulder down to his right armpit, blood spurted out and coated Marlon's face, causing him to close his eyes and laugh. Joseph howled again in agony and Scarlett quickly connected on the side of his head with the hilt of her sword, Joseph's vision swam, Marlon was in doubles and his collapsed to the ground. The world swam around him but he managed a grin when he heard a bang and saw Marlon's eyes go wide, a red blooming wound spreading out on the left side of his chest.

He collapsed to the ground and lay beside Joseph, his eyes wide and unseeing. Scarlett turned and called out, "No, wait stop! I hated him and I'm glad he's dead, I was only following orders, you don't need to kill me." Anne ran forward, more a blur of red hair and clothes than anything else.

Scarlett made a dive for Marlon's gun, dropping her dull sword. With the last of his strength Joseph managed to get up on one knee, drawing his trusty wooden daggers, he slammed both into either side of her throat, collapsing on top of her.

"Sure we don't have to kill you, but you deserve it. Following orders is what the Nazi's did. Rot in hell Scarlett!"

She tried to howl in pain but only managed to vomit blood all over Joseph. She back fisted him in the head and everything went black.

***

Joseph woke up in Anne's arms. She was licking the blood off his chest and moved up to his face. Cassandra had done the same for him and he had grown to like it. He closed his eyes and then gritted his teeth with the pain. Everything was sore, he could feel his bones already starting to mend but knew it would take hours, the wound on his chest would be even longer, the blade must be silver. He opened his eyes and carefully looked from side to side, Scarlett's decapitated body lie on the ground next to her own severed head, all that was left of Marlon was his clothes, weapon and duffle bag, his body ash.

"You saved me, th-thank you." His voice was only a whisper.

Anne laughed, "This turned into quite a first date didn't it?"

Joseph's paranoid mind starting churning, "Their phones, the Countess will expect them to check in, give a report."

Anne laid Joseph down on the ground, he grimaced with the pain in his ribs, foot and hand but kept his eyes open.

She found both phones and crushed them in their hands. "Problem solved, no phones."

"Well we may have found information on them but yeah it does solve the problem, thanks again. Collect up their stuff, can't leave it here. And of course the body, you'll have to throw Scarlett out in the ocean."

Anne gathered the weapons and flung them in the duffle bag. "By we, you mean me." She stood with her hands on her hips.

Joseph managed to get up on one elbow. "I can't walk on this foot, at least not until the bones heal and I don't think we should wait. That was a lot of noise and the cops or people from nearby could should up soon."

Anne sighed, "All right you're got a point. Keep an eye out and give some stay away thoughts, I'll tidy up. I found their rowboat, I can put some holes in it and push it out to sea, which will get rid of Scarlett."

Joseph nodded, he could already feel his foot and wiggled a toe, regeneration was a wonderful thing. "Will do, it was my left foot so I can drive back to the house. You're welcome to stay with me tonight, it's the least I can do. I just need help getting in the car."

Anne busied herself with the tasks, holding up a hand. "Thanks for the offer but I still need time to think, especially after what just happened."

The Countess has crossed a line, threatening not just me but one of my best friends, I can't just continue to be a pawn. I need to find a way to strike at the Council, a way to stop her from fucking up my life and hurting the ones I care about. Joseph forced himself up on his knees, he urged and released the contents of his stomach. *I still hate the sight of a dead body, I hope it's something I never get used to.*

Chapter 12: Halloween Homecoming

Joseph drove home from Topsail Beach, it was past midnight and no cars passed him on the other side, no one behind him either. He knew his head, foot and ribs would be almost better in the morning but they still smarted like hell. His chest burned, *silver made the wounds bleed longer than usual, have to use rubbing alcohol to clean it and even then it will take a day or so. That old sweater in the back seat had come in handy, and it was red.*

He rubbed the bridge of his nose. *How did my life become so complicated?* He had some kind of casual sex arrangement with Roxanne, something else maybe with Anne, his parents came back soon, he was trying to finishing up his degree and of course he had no idea when the Council would send lackeys after him again or threaten someone else he cared about. As if all that wasn't enough, he knew that someday, maybe within the next year, he would be fighting for his life in some kind of crazy war.

I could sure as hell use a drink. He felt so stressed, he let out a sigh, and he winced as his healing ribs protested the movement. *I need something to take my mind off everything,* so he flicked through his iPhone, scanning for a song to give him a little solace and advice. He stumbled on "The Sunscreen Song" and hit play. He had loved this song for years and much of it still held true.

Don't worry about the future

Joseph could agree; the future would come soon enough. For now it was best just to focus on the present, on the return of his parents. He had a gun in the house and another in the trunk along with the crossbow. He would have to hide them well, while his parents knew he had a love of swords, they would be shocked and perhaps even call the police over guns. As he pulled into Cherry Lane, the lyrics delivered a little more for him to ponder on...

Don't be reckless with other people's hearts

He snickered at the floss line, that sure didn't matter anymore but everything else did. Anne had made no promises about a relationship or love, neither had Roxanne. Both women told him the truth, as far as he could tell. It was Cassandra who shattered his trust and broke his heart, she was the one he had to make peace with. He had never liked much time alone but someday he might have to face many years of it, if he survived the coming battle.

For now though his cats, a warm bed and a little tidying up before his parents got home awaited him. He recalled that tomorrow afternoon in English class Dr. Miller was about to start talking about *Dracula* by Bram Stoker and that would be interesting and fun, now more so than ever.

* * *

Joseph felt like crap up in the day, even worse with his still healing and very tender chest. His new cat Jude was sleeping patiently at the foot of his bed helped his mood lighten. It was past 11am and he had to get moving. He had classes at one, three and five today. His last four courses for his degree, he hoped this time he would get a chance to finish them. He arranged some candy it in a bowl and left it outside with a note that said "Halloween candy! Please have some but consider others." Whether anyone took it all or none didn't matter to him. It would be too weird to be home handing out candy as a vampire so he would just stay out in town until he had to get his parents tonight at the airport.

He remembered the guns and crossbow, they had to go out of sight. Even though he had a room in residence it was too risky there, nowhere good to hide them. He walked to the old shed at the back of their land, once used as a stable. Pulling open the door he found some towels and carefully wrapped the weapons up. Walking around he heard a creak and pulled up a loose floorboard, placing the guns under it. He could not imagine anyone ever looking there and even if someone did, he had wiped off prints to be certain.

He took the van this time as his parents would have luggage. He put his sword under the seat and checked for his wooden daggers, never did he imagine when he bought them a couple of years ago in martial arts that they would be used to kill. *What is Anne doing today? Roxanne too, does either of them think about me? What is happening with Cassandra and the Countess? I told her about the fight with the vampires last night, but I left out how hurt and embarrassed I was. We all have secrets and I'm sure she'll tell me what is going on in Paris in due time.*

He smiled, life wasn't so bad. He figured he had a reasonable chance of having fun with at least one woman tonight and he'd have to learn to enjoy the present and not worry so much about the future. Of course he did see that he would need to get better with this expanding rod, he may have to fight two opponents again soon. Once as his chest felt better he would practice.

* * *

Anne was putting on the last part of her costume, a pair of long black leather boots, and black stockings. *The cape is a bit much but I like the boots and the collar. Joseph was good last night, Cassandra has taught him about pleasing a woman. He is also becoming quite the warrior, I could have intervened sooner but he needs to be strong, he has to fight through pain and injuries if what he says is true, a war is coming.*

The Newfoundland Vampire   Charles O'Keefe

She shivered at the thought. *So much for my peace and isolation, this Countess sounds like one nasty, evil bitch and she means business. Joseph is right, if she's screwing with him and Cassandra, I'll be next.*

She applied some eyeliner and lipstick, smiling at herself in the mirror. *If my plan is going to work, then I am going to need a lot more info about this Countess. For tonight though, I'm a little hungry for something else. I do need a night out before all this serious business. It will be easy to find a lassie or laddie in this getup and a girl does need to eat.* Anne finished her makeup and left her hotel room. She loved Halloween. It was the only day of the year she could let her fangs down and no one would care.

* * *

Joseph managed to stay awake for philosophy class, barely. It's not that he didn't acknowledge the wage inequality between men and women as important, it shouldn't be there at all, but it was hard to be awake and alert during the day. He had sent Roxanne a text message, just asking if she wanted to hang out tonight for a bit, *anything to take my mind off of all the stress.* He did hope to be with Anne again too. Sex with a vampire was so much better than with a human and he wanted to be regaled by Anne's exploits. He also wanted to know if she had the same jaded view of humanity that Cassandra held. A life far longer than a human lifespan didn't equate to a jaded personality, it couldn't always be the case. Before he knew it he was headed to English class.

He had loved the whole course; *Frankenstein, Jekyll and Hyde*, some vampire short stories and now *Dracula*. The irony and fun of a vampire going to a class about what everyone thought was a work of fiction, and on Halloween, was very high. *If only she knew the truth.* He walked in the class room, it was 5pm and the sun was low in the sky. His body told him it was less than an hour to sunset, but that didn't help the pounding headache and the creeping tiredness in his limbs.

Dr. Miller walked into the classroom. She had a cape on and Joseph immediately smiled. He was wearing his Star Trek uniform and a few other people wore costumes as well.

She said, "Well isn't this fun? Talking about old Bram and Dracula on Halloween? I hope all of you had a chance to read the book."

Joseph found with his nocturnal nature he got through a book a lot quicker. The students settled and most took out iPads and laptops, though a few still used pen and paper. Joseph was old school and still used a paper and pen.

Dr. Miller continued, "I'm glad to see some of you dressed for the occasion. As most of you know, I have devoted much of the last nine years of my life to showing that Bram Stoker did not base Dracula on Vlad the Impaler. In fact the only connection we know for sure is that he used Vlad's last name, Dracula, which meant son of Dracul, or in English, son of the dragon. "

Joseph listened intently, most of the class was about how Vlad the Impaler was never meant to be Dracula. Eventually she began to talk about the plot of the book and then Transylvania and the real Dracula castle. Joseph knew the truth about the real Dracula and shivered a little when he imagined what he could be doing now.

Joseph's mind raced, *who had he portrayed in history? What kind of horrible council business was he doing now? Did Bram Stoker have any notion that vampires existed? Had he ever met one?* He chuckled to himself at that last thought and Dr. Miller turned to him.

135

The Newfoundland Vampire   Charles O'Keefe

"Joseph, right? Something funny about Bram or the old Count?"

Joseph was a little embarrassed but he covered as best he could. "Oh sorry, I was wondering what Bram Stoker would say about all the modern day interpretations of vampires. Twilight, the count from Sesame Street, the old Bela Lugosi movies, even Count Chocula cereal, it's amusing what popular culture has done to Dracula."

She nodded, "Well you bring up a good point. The image of the vampire has certainly changed a lot over time. Mr. Stoker wouldn't say much about Twilight, so neither will I. As for the movie called *Bram Stoker's Dracula*, well it didn't hold true to his writing, at least not often. The other merchandise, it's hard to say, the world wasn't such a commercial place in 1897. As for others, I think that turning any vampire book into a movie or television show is taking a risk of it looking silly, at least by our modern standards. One of the only good adaptations of Dracula was done in 1977 by the BBC, I'll show that in a later class."

Joseph couldn't resist asking a question that popped into his head, "What would Bram Stoker say about an Anne Rice type vampire, one with full control of their emotions and able to make choices about what kind of blood they drink?"

Dr. Miller laughed a little continuing, "Someone has put a lot of thought into this! While Mr. Stoker certainly associated vampires as more sexual than humans, I'm not sure if he would have liked them as such depressed and moody creatures. Louis is rather pathetic as a vampire if I recall. Now Lestat probably would be more of a character Mr. Stoker would have liked." Glancing at her watch she said, "Well that's it for today, Have a happy Halloween everyone and watch out for things that go bump in the night!"

The students chuckled, collected their belongings and left. Joseph couldn't resist staying behind to ask a couple more questions. He walked up to her and said, "You've gone to Transylvania. What do the locals say about their famous vampire?"

"I have been there, quite interesting for sure. A lot of tourists coming looking for backward villagers but it's actually now the most successful and modern part of Romania. Of course tourism groups want to capitalize on the Count. Most people like tourists and only get annoyed if you act like vampires exist and expect them to point one out!" She chuckled.

Joseph couldn't help having fun, the sheer irony of the situation was so present in his mind. "Sure I guess a lot of places just tolerate tourists and stereotypes. How about Vlad's castle? That must be a creepy place."

She finished packing her notes and walked towards the door. "You should go there sometime. Yes, Vlad Tepes' castle is there. It's mostly in ruins now but I wouldn't want to be there at night. Even during the day it was creepy; I heard wolves howling in the distance. With that note you go off and have a happy Halloween!" She wrapped her cloak around herself and walked off.

Joseph laughed and called out, "Thanks, you too!" *If only Dr. Miller, if only you knew.*

He dug out his phone and saw that Roxanne had replied, *Sure Joe, I'm at the Yellowbelly now for a few hours having a bite with some friends, come down and join me if you'd like, later!*

That would be good, he wrote back 'ok I'll see you there soon.'

Before heading downtown, he had to have his own bite to eat. Luckily he had brought a change of clothes.

The Newfoundland Vampire   Charles O'Keefe

* * *

With his stomach full of moose blood, Joseph headed downtown. After last night he searched out for other vampires, thankfully he only felt one. This time instead of scared and anxious he was just a little nervous, he knew it was Anne. After they drank each other's blood it gave them a connection and he could sense her thoughts, somewhat. *I'll be with you soon Joseph. It's going to be a fun night*, she sent.

It was a cold night, almost cold enough to snow, but the sky was clear and lots of people milled about. He parked the van down by the waterfront and headed up. He wanted to bring his sword, it should be with him all the time, but there would be cops and extra security and there was just no way tonight, he settled on the silver dagger from last night in his coat. He loved costumes and all the ones around now made him smile. He felt, to some extent, he was always pretending to be someone else, at least when he was around humans.

Some costumes included *Ted*, *Batman*, *Thor*, *Hulk* and several Daenerys from *Game of Thrones*. Other costumes looked much more bizarre like a guy as a huge toilet seat cover and several people with grey ties, a whip and handcuffs. Joseph thought that he may just not be hip enough to get some of the references.

I'm not cold, but some of these women hardly wear anything, they must be freezing. One particular *Wonder Woman* outfit left nothing to the imagination and Joseph certainly hoped she would win some kind of prize. He stopped staring, it was rude and her *Superman* boyfriend glared at him.

Paying the cover charge, he got his wristband, and ventured onto George Street. He leisurely strolled by O'Reily's, Kelly's, Turkey Joe's and others. Music spilled out from every bar, some of it Halloween themed, others played Irish and folk music, still others horrible dance music and a couple had live bands. Throngs of people jammed up George Street and he found he had to slow down or squeeze by groups several times. His mind was assaulted by all of their thoughts, the noise and the smells, often none too pleasant. He did his best to focus and soon found himself at the end of the street.

"Leaving already?" one of the ticket guys asked.

"Only to get in Yellowbelly, I guess I can't get in the back way."

The man smiled as he took people's money and handed them wristbands, "Nope sorry pal, have a good night though."

Joseph nodded and soon found himself in Yellowbelly. It was crowded here too. He soon spotted Roxanne. She was wearing a red fedora type hat, her hair in two long braids, a green bathing suit, green painted stripes on each leg and blue boots. She was a lovely, sexy woman, even more so in this costume. She smiled and said "Hi Joe!" she ran up and gave him a hug.

Joseph returned the friendly gesture and added a kiss on the cheek.

She scanned him up and down, "I know you're Star Trek, red shirt I guess?"

Joseph laughed, a red-shirt meant a character in Star Trek who died quickly and for little reason.

"I hadn't thought of that but sure, red-shirt is a good one. Actually, I'm just a huge geek who owns a Star Trek uniform. I know who you are, great costume!"

She laughed this time and did a little spin, "Thanks! So then smarty, spit it out."

Joseph had played video games a lot when he was young, still did a little bit on his iPad. He knew it was a character from Street Fighter. "I know it's Street Fighter, I used to play video games a lot and Super Nintendo was the first system I had. Cammy, right?"

"Yeah it's Street Fighter and Cammy. She's from the UK but I can't pull off the accent. My friends left and I waited for you, so buy me a drink!"

Joseph smiled and thought, *she's in a good mood. If I didn't have to go to the airport soon there could be another fun night with her.* "Of course, I'll get us a both a drink, beer?" Just as the words left his mouth when he felt Anne's presence very close by, mere seconds away.

"Yeah sure, I'm not a fancy drink girl. Whatever's on tap is good."

Joseph went to the bar and got them both a beer, one of the house brews, he wasn't too concerned which one. He, along with a lot of other patrons he was sure, looked up as Anne come into the bar. She wore a long red cape with black trim and a black studded collar. Her hair was pinned up and she wore a red bodice that pushed her breasts up. She wore long black leather boots and most shockingly her fangs protruded out and her eyes glowed red! She was sexy and hot but he was worried, he couldn't help it.

Roxanne walked over to Joseph to get her beer. "She's a looker huh? She went to a lot of trouble with the fangs and red contact lenses."

Anne was getting several stares and Joseph caught snatches of the thoughts of those in the bar, *check out the fangs on her, those eyes . . . creepy, that's one hot vamp, I'd like to grab that collar and. . .*

Anne laughed and smiled, she enjoyed the attention, and slowly sauntered towards them.

"Greetings chum, I see you've already bought this fine lass a drink, how about one for me?"

Joseph gulped and nodded, laying his drink down. "Oh…um…sure I'd be happy too."

Roxanne smiled, "Hey cool costume, I like your boots. So you know Joseph?"

Joseph thought to Anne, *Fangs and red eyes? You even a little concerned someone might suspect it's not a costume?*

Anne thought back, *Lighten up! Its Halloween laddie, the only night we can let our true nature show a little.* "Thanks hon. Yes I got into town a few nights ago. Joseph took me for a nice walk down on the beach, after he showed me a thing or two with his sword." She winked at Joseph and Roxanne narrowed her eyes at him.

Joseph spoke up, "Oh, I'm sorry. Roxanne this is Anne Bonny. Roxanne is someone I know from Memorial, we're friends."

Anne extended her hand and Roxanne shook it, "Pleased to meet you Anne, Joseph hasn't told me about using a sword, he's full of surprises tonight. Anne Bonny, you mean like the pirate? That's a cool coincidence."

Joseph had a feeling she was upset but he couldn't help himself, he wanted to know for sure, so he snooped on Roxanne's mind. *We might have become more than friends but not if he's going to be with other women. Sword practice, that's subtle. I'll finish my drink and find my friends, Joseph obviously has his hands full with her tonight.*

Anne gulped her beer and glanced at the two of them. "Thank you. You have quite the figure but, I have no idea who you're supposed to be. I suppose I'm a little out of touch."

Roxanne drank her beer a little faster. Joseph put his head down and frowned. *As a vampire I'll always have trouble with human relationships, I can't be mad at Anne, she didn't force me to do anything.* He checked his watch and saw that it was almost ten, it's not like he could stay long anyway. He took a big gulp of his beer as well.

Roxanne stepped closer to Anne, "Well it's from a video game, Street Fighter. Joseph knew it but he's a huge geek, so don't feel bad. I have to ask, can I touch your fangs? They look so real! How did you get them on?"

Anne put down her drink and tilted her head forward, "Yes of course lassie, be careful though they're quite sharp. I used dental glue, it keeps them on tight for about five days." Joseph felt Anne's thoughts again, *we'll talk after she's left.*

Joseph finished his beer and just nodded to Anne. Roxanne carefully examined her fangs. Anne was smart enough to close her eyes, that close a person could tell she wasn't wearing contacts.

Roxanne stepped back and finished her beer. "Pretty cool, I'll have to check online for them. Well it was nice meeting you Anne." She turned and gave Joseph a quick kiss on the cheek, whispering in his ear, "Thanks for the drink and have a fun night."

Joseph briefly laid a hand on her arm, "You're welcome, have a happy Halloween and I'll see you soon." Roxanne walked away.

Anne moved closer to him and whispered. "She's got a nice ass huh? She was friendly too, for a human."

Joseph spoke softly, he knew Anne could focus on even a whisper. "Yeah she's attractive, but for a human? That's a pretty snide remark."

Anne gulped her beer and motioned for two more, she spoke softly as well, "Fine Joseph, but you do need to lighten up. You also need to accept that you're not human. Any relationship you have with them is fleeting."

Joseph started working on his second beer and replied, "Thanks for the beer. As for humans, I happen to disagree.

I am still very human in many ways, I want to have human relationships. My parents, friends, family, Roxanne, they all matter to me. We live on a planet with billions of them, I don't see the point in shutting them out. You talk a lot like Cassandra, dismissing humans as unimportant."

Anne smiled, appreciating a few lingering stares from people in the bar. "I talk like her because she's right. Oh and I figured it out, you're having sex with this Roxanne. Cassandra and I had an orgy with three men the other night. Combining all the blood together was delicious."

She turned to face him, her eyes peering up into his. "You'll see over the next fifty years how different it will be. Your parents and family will be mostly gone, your friends will lose importance to you and your whole outlook will change. Humans can be fun. They serve a purpose and many in turn serve us. We're the dominant species in this world and I don't see the point in developing connections with anyone who will only be around for the blink of an eye. Let's walk and talk as they say, don't worry we'll switch to telepathy."

Joseph downed the rest of his beer, he wasn't in the mood to hang out in this crowded bar anymore. Anne had spoken some truths he would one day have to accept. He wanted some air. He went outside and Anne followed, none too quickly, but she came out. His breath made little puffs in the air and Anne's did the same, his ribs had healed and breathing no longer hurt. He sent to Anne, *thank you again for last night, I don't know how I can repay you.*

Anne thought back, *you're welcome lad, I want you to know I only waited that long to help to make you strong, you told me of what is to come. For now, though, we have more pressing matters to discuss, like when I can wrap my lips around your...*

Joseph turned red, he was still shy sometimes, "Anne please, we're in public." *I knew she waited last night! I'm glad she wasn't the one to train me, she certainly believes in a trial by fire.*

Anne was laughing, it was warm and pleasant. He smiled despite himself and she did the same, *I'm just having some fun with you lad. Now I know it won't happen tonight, you're learning about hiding your deeper secrets but I am aware you have to go to the airport soon.*

Joseph thought back, *what is it with every vampire I have sex with prying into my mind? Cassandra always said it was unintentional but if we're going to be in a relationship I need…*

Hold your horses there Joe. I'm having fun with you and I'd like to for a little while longer but I don't want some big commitment. A relationship is a human notion and I've moved past it. Those thoughts of your parents bubbled right on the surface. The difference between you, me, Cassandra and I assume you meant the Countess, was that while we love the sensation of mixing vampire blood together, it's not all consuming. Just like I ran my nails up and down your back during sex, I glanced over your mind. You need to take it as a compliment, someone is enjoying themselves enough that they want to know you a little better, you could have done so with me too.

They had just walked past Atlantic Place, passing restaurants and stores as they continued along Water Street.

Joseph let out a long breath, *okay I'm sorry, I have some trust issues, though with good reason. Sure I get it, I guess most vampires don't date or act like couples.*

Anne giggled a little, *date? I haven't heard that word used in such a long time, cute one my lad. Time to get serious though, after last night   I came up with plan in mind to hurt this council, take away the control and fear they have over us. Believe it or not, a small part of that plan involves nail polish, hair color and maybe a little makeup.*

Joseph headed down a short tunnel and Anne followed. He mulled over Anne's idea. A plan was exciting and fascinated him, he knew the Count and Countess as pure evil and he wanted to bring them both down, especially after the brutal fight last night. "I agree Anne, I can't pretend the Council doesn't affect my life. I want to strike back, if we can do so without getting killed naturally."

"Oh well naturally. I've lived for over three centuries, I'd hope to be around for at least a wee bit more."

Joseph checked his watch and saw he had a few more minutes before he'd have to go to the airport. *I do love her accent and her sense of humor.* He snickered as they approached the van.

"Like that one huh? I know you'd certainly like to live past the ripe old age of twenty-three." She winked at him.

He smiled and hurried ahead. Ever the gentleman he opened the van door for Anne and she got in.

Anne continued, "I know you need to go. For now I just ask two favors, let me see into your mind and get a clear glimpse of the Countess, just what her appearance is now. That and contact Cassandra. Find out what she's doing with this foul murderer and get all the information you can from her. I'll need both your help and I hope you'll agree. I'll see you soon, here's my e-mail and cell number just in case."

Anne handed Joseph a card and he pocked it. He fished out a sticky pad from his coat pocket, wrote his cell and e-mail on it and passed it to Anne. "I'll share what I know of the Countess, I got to know her quite well from a three-way I was forced to have with her and Cassandra."

Anne snorted and covered her mouth, Joseph frowned.

"Sorry dear, I just find it a little hard to believe any man could be forced into a three-way. Please continue."

"I'll talk this over with Cassandra. I'm certain that she isn't just hanging out with the Countess. The Countess forced her to help, probably to protect me. I want you to know I care for you and trust you. "

Anne nodded and leaned over to give him a long, soulful kiss while stroking the back of his head and neck. Joseph took the clip out of her hair and caressed it. Resisting locks of long red hair was something he could never do.

She pulled back and smiled, "Please contact me soon. I'm trusting you as well. This war is coming and if we don't act soon it may be too late to act. Enjoy your time with your parents. If you would like for me to meet them I'd be happy to. Explain me anyway you want."

Joseph replied, "I'll think about it. Here's what you wanted about the Countess." He held up his hand and Anne took his index finger in her mouth, sucking at first, licking it and then biting to start the embrace.

Joseph felt himself getting hard already, despite the pain. She held her wrist up to him and he carefully bit into the underside of it. The blood was exquisite, he knew she had drank from a person earlier but he didn't care, it was a moment of pleasure in his frazzled state of affairs. He thought of that night, the two women kissing and caressing, the Countess and her slim figure and flat abs, her small breasts and whip straight brown hair, her high cheekbones and exotic features, her Hungarian accent he found so sexy at first, all of the pleasant aspects and he was rock hard.

Anne snapped her fangs up, cleaned off the blood and took his finger out of her mouth, Joseph also stopped the blood flow and cleaned her wrist in return.

She rubbed her hand over his crotch, "Not all bad memories I see. Thank you for that."

Joseph opened his eyes and said, "Umm…could you…I mean can we…"

Anne winked and opened the van door, half getting out, "Not tonight horny toad. Dream of me. Maybe you'll even get another three-way?" She laughed and added "You never did closely see all my freckles. Look after yourself landlubber."

"You're welcome and ahh, you too, except the landlubber part."

Her laughter faded away as he started the van and put it in drive. Thoughts swirled around his head. *Her talking about acting now and wanting an image of the Countess means only one thing, she wants to kill the Countess with our help. What else could it be?* He would contact Cassandra soon. For now he needed to push all of the Council business aside and act as normal as possible, he had to be strong. He felt more than ever that his time with his parents was finite.

Pulling up to the airport, he parked the car and headed in. It was 10:55pm, he had just made it. Getting to bottom of the escalator, he waited. He let his mind go blank and just concentrated. He knew he could make his skin less pale, maybe it wouldn't show tonight. He loved his parents dearly and he did miss them the past six weeks. His Mom often said she wouldn't be around forever but he had always dismissed the idea. Passengers began to arrive and he saw his dad first. He had a blue jacket, a red, white and blue-checkered shirt underneath and a white baseball cap, now faded and yellowed with age, his usual beige pants and brown docksiders. His mom had on a white jacket, a green sweater, black slacks, white tennis shoes and of course, her usual sun visor with sunglasses perched on top of her head, despite the fact it was nighttime. They both appeared tired but his dad smiled and his mom waved as they saw him. He waved back.

His mom kissed and hugged him while his dad waited and gave him a handshake. "We missed you," His mom said.

Joseph replied, "I missed you both too, welcome back."

Chapter 13: Son of the Dragon

The Count wandered the tourist area of Sighişoara, Transylvania. He hadn't returned to the area in many years and tonight, Halloween, he just couldn't resist coming back. It was a nice little town, nestled in the valley. It reminded him of when the world was a simpler place and he could kill with impunity. It was snowing a little but that didn't stop tourists on their Halloween tours. He wore a long coat with a fur collar and black boots that he kept from his time as Adolf, his old sword, the killij, even his hand cannon. Normally carrying large weapons would attract attention, maybe even get him arrested, but tonight he fit right in. He listened to the thoughts of those around him, the normal crap about drinking, sex, TV, worries about work and money. Some people dressed as vampires, some people as bizarre turtle men and even a few as some kind of a robot with a sword, they would all die later.

Standing by the statue of Vlad near the city hall he read when the world thought he died, 1476. *Five-hundred years, so much time has passed. They got the mustache right, though the face was a little off. I do enjoy coming back here, they still view Vlad as a hero, despite everything I did and my brutality, fools.* He thought of Vlad's last days and his mood soured. He gritted his teeth and spat, speaking out loud "Fucking Emperor! Always meddling!" *Even back then he screwed up my life. He decided my time was done as Vlad and I had to follow suit, had to move on and then let some hapless lookalike be killed and beheaded.*

He focused back on the good times, *those were the days, the impalements, the blood, the glory of battle, it will all come again soon,* and he smiled to himself. *My dear Commodus wants me to make thralls, those who would serve him but they will only serve me. I have hidden in the shadows too long. I will rule them all and the Emperor will meet his end!*

Walking along the cobblestone steps he snarled at anyone who got close and occasionally flashed his red eyes or fangs just to get a jolt out of some hapless fool. Soon he happened upon a bright yellow stone building. The faded letters read,

"Casa Vlad Draclu" on the side of the building. What bothered him was a pathetic wooden statue of a vampire which proclaimed "visit the room where Dracula was born." The vampire was black, red and white, had a moronic cap, bat like ears, and fangs much too large to be useful.

He made fists and gritted his teeth, *they want to trivialize me and turn me into a joke! These stupid humans have gone too far, Vlad was born here and he was a man I admired, before I killed and became him. This desecrates his memory and only helps to popularize what fucking Hollywood did to Bram's story. Bram never knew me, never even went to Transylvania but he wrote a good yarn. It's where I got the notion to call myself the Count after all.*

A smaller note underneath it said, *Come in and you might get a visit from the Count himself!* At this Count laughed, more of horrible cackle. "Oh you're all about to get a visit all right. I'll give them a Halloween they'll never forget." He turned on his phone and quickly sent a text, for a little while longer he would follow the Emperor's rules. He wrote, *in Sighișoara, send a cleanup crew and do your job, I'm about to rip this place up.*

He knew there would be some moron who would video this massacre and his appearance was still too much like Osama for that to work, so he slipped from his cloak a new creation. He had made a mask of bone, the skull was much larger than his own and he could almost fit the whole thing over his head. Only his eyes, nose, and the bottom part of his mouth where visible.

If only the Countess where here to share in the destruction, where is my creation? Reaching out with his mind while he tightened the straps on his mask he felt nothing. *The lack of her presence is disturbing and I miss her joy for killing. I shall find her soon.*

Striding through the restaurant door he saw the place was about half-full. A waitress wearing fake fangs and dark eye makeup greeted him nervously. She spoke with a Romanian accent that was not as strong as in years gone by, "Good evening Sir. That's quite a costume you have. Table for one?"

The Count had to do one last thing, he used his considerable telepathy to project to everyone present, *this is a show for Halloween, no need to be alarmed.*

Once the terror set upon their feeble minds it would be all the sweeter. "You want to have a visit from the Count?" he called out loudly, ignoring the woman's question. "The Count is here you stupid bastards!"

The woman blinked and her eyes widened as his hand shot forward and he grasped her by the throat. With ease, he lifted her off her feet and flung her toward the nearest table. People began to point and several started to get their phones and cameras out. The manager, who was wearing a Lugosi style vampire outfit, quickly came over and whispered to him intently, "I know this is a show but take it easy on my staff we don't want anyone to get…"

"Silence fool!" the Count yelled as he head-butted him in the mouth, breaking his jaw, nose, most of his teeth and knocking him to the floor. People began to clap and call out. Flashes went off and the Count was certain several videos would be taken.

I'll give them a show that will be the stuff of nightmares.

The Newfoundland Vampire   Charles O'Keefe

Another man from behind the bar approached. The suggestion was not strong enough for him to ignore the blood and teeth on the floor.

He approached the Count holding a knife before him, "Someone call the police! This isn't a…"

The Count moved too fast for any human eye to follow. He leaped forward and drew his kilij, slicing upwards and carving the man in two halves. Blood, guts and brains drenched the Count. His fangs came down and he licked the blood in pleasure. People finally began to run for the exit but, incredibly, a few remained, either frozen in terror or somehow still believing this to be a show.

The Count saw one man, wearing a shirt that said "Vegetarian vampire" still holding up his phone, his face drained of color but he was unable to move. Reaching to the other side of his cloak, the Count pulled out the hand cannon, a smoke and powder weapon over five-hundred years old. Laying his sword briefly on the bar, he used a match to light the powder, pointed and fired. The ball hit the man in the gut and he fell to the ground. People screamed. The Count retrieved his sword and searched for another victim. He found a woman, also with a vampire shirt that had the words "Twilight Breaking Dawn" on it. He grabbed her, and before she could scream reached into her mouth and ripped out her tongue. Putting away his weapons, he grabbed both the injured man and woman and flung one over each shoulder. A cop stood outside on the street, his gun drawn. He wore a blue uniform with a black peaked black hat, he had on black leather coat over his uniform with brown fur around the collar. He stood near a white van with "politia" written on the side. The Count gave him a dismissive frown and flashed his eyes red. A crowd had gathered outside, *I couldn't give a shit, let the Council clean it up.*

He lowered the two people on his shoulders to the ground. A bead of sweat trickled down the police officer's forehead despite the cold.

"Don't move! The whole station is on the…"

The Count roared in defiance and retrieved a dagger from his boot, throwing it in a split second. The blade lodged deep in the cop's throat. The man instinctively reached for the dagger as blood gurgled from his mouth ran down his chin. The Count knew the fun was over and collected up the two on the ground and put one on each shoulder again. *They will do fine as thralls.* Moving now with as much speed as he could manage while carrying two people, he quickly found his way to the woods and out of sight.

The night is young and Zagar is not far away, it's Halloween after all and I'll give them the real Count for a change.

Chapter 14: Vampire en Francis

Cassandra enjoyed the view of the lights of Paris. She was at the top of the Eiffel tower, illegally as it was long past visiting hours. She was lost in the events earlier in the evening when she felt a familiar presence enter her mind. Like the rotating light on top of the tower, it was something that was hard to ignore. She knew it was Joseph, his sweet manner came through even telepathically.

Can we talk? I had an important…ah…conversation with Anne that you need to hear about.

Cassandra sighed. She had just gotten through the unpleasantness dealing with her French contact, Louis D'Enfer, out of her head, *what a lecherous buffoon, merely a puppet for the Countess. Passing his loyalty test was easy, if unpleasant.* The quiet and stillness from up here helped, but she knew Joseph would not contact her unless it was important. So she replied, *yes of course dear one and please don't take me for naïve, you're a young, horny vampire, I know you did more than just talk. I know she could satisfy me handily, how does she do with a man?*

There was a pause and then his reply. It felt hesitant but then poured in. *Well…um yes we did, you're right about blood, it's the only way for us to achieve real pleasure and I had to be a part of her memories to make certain she was telling the truth. And yeah she's good, she doesn't know me like you do but we had fun. She's obviously bisexual. More importantly though, Anne has a plan to kill the Countess and to infiltrate the Council.*

Cassandra smiled at this. Even though it still stung that he was enjoying sex with another woman, he softened the blow and still knew what to say to her. She sat down on the floor and closed her eyes, concentrating to make sure she got every word and nuance of this mental conversation.

Proceed beloved, you have my attention. Since I'm here because of the Countess, we do need to strike a blow for our side, if for no other reason than to get her and the Council off our backs.

I couldn't agree more. The last time I met with Anne, she wanted a complete picture of the Countess. She wants the three of us to kill the Countess and she will take her place. If we keep her alive, the three of us can force our way into her mind, get her whole history and learn everything we need to know in order for Anne to impersonate her.

Cassandra opened her eyes for a moment, the idea was shocking and yet very clever. She had never forced another vampire to share memories but the three of them together could quite possibly force any memories out of her, especially if the Countess had lost blood from a fight and was in a weakened state. *We will have to plumb the depths of her soul, see all the depraved and horrible acts she has done in her long life. Can you handle this? More importantly, when you linked with Anne she was telling the whole truth? While memories cannot lie, she could still have secrets, a hidden agenda mayhap. We're putting both of our lives in her hands Joseph, you have to be certain.*

Cassandra could almost sense a slow nod. She giggled, she couldn't help it. Despite the seriousness of the conversation it was cute.

I'm as certain as possible. She shared with me how her creator, John Roberts beat her within an inch of her life and would have killed her had the navy not shown up. Robert's gave her a choice of joining the Council or dying. Why would she share this if it's not true? She strikes me as someone who values her freedom and privacy, the Council threatens both. We're helping the Council win, not by choice but still we must not let it continue. Anne wants the Countess gone just as much as we do, if for no other reason than to avoid becoming a slave to the Council and forced to do unspeakable acts. They will get to me too and I . . . I can't take much more. If I have to know the memories to bring down the Countess, no matter how disgusting and evil, then I'll do it. It has to be done and this is the time.

The Newfoundland Vampire   Charles O'Keefe

Cassandra had doubts about Joseph's maturity sometimes. She had doubted if he had the right attitude toward immortally and even towards the human race but he was right about this. The Countess was rotten to the core and just like her creator and Donald, she had to go.

Cassandra furrowed her brow, *why now? Everything else you say rings true but why not take time to weigh all our options? Learn more about Anne and the Countess and do it at a time when the Countess is most vulnerable and we're most prepared?*

The answer is the ring. If you remember when she showed up we could not sense her presence. She boasted about the magic ring that she wore. Anne pointed out that the ring could have a significant drawback, it could also cut off all communication she has with other vampires. Cut her off even from the Count and any creations she made. Find this out, trick her into talking about the ring's properties. She may not have the ring on for much longer and then our best chance to get her is gone.

Cassandra pensively rested her chin on her hand, *once again you and Anne make some valid points. I will do my best to determine if the ring does have this property and that she is still wearing it. The only flaw in the plan is this: why would the Countess leave Paris and follow me? Surely she has pressing business and there's no guarantee you could both make it to Paris before she leaves.*

Convince her to come to St. Pierre. Anne has connections there and has prepared an old building for us to kill her in. She showed me through her memories and I have to agree it's perfect. More importantly, Anne is the one that got away. If you tell the Countess that Anne is willing to join and I'm ready to accept my next assignment, I'm certain she will come. Her pride won't let her say no. She'll want to be the one to finally get a three-hundred year old vampire to their side. It will be a chance for her to show up this John Roberts.

Cassandra weaved her hands through her hair, getting out a few tangles, and pulled it back into a ponytail. *It all make senses and if Anne trusts Joseph and me that much, well, I have to believe in her intentions.* She sent out back to Joseph, *I will do everything I can to convince her and to make certain the ring stays with her.*

Cassandra's phone beeped, it was a text from the Countess. *Meet with me at Hotel De La Trémoille at 5am top floor, bring three live humans. Don't even consider running, you would pray for death when I'm finished with you.*

Cassandra closed her eyes and rubbed her forehead, she began to sob. Three more victims to this monstrous cause. Hardening herself, she resumed the conversation. *That Countess bitch just contacted me again, I have to bring three victims to her soon. Let's bring her down once and for all, I can't live like this. No matter the consequences and even if Anne is less than forthwith, we have to risk it. Come up with an explanation for your family and get to St. Pierre. I will do my best and let you know.*

Joseph's reply came instantly, *we'll be ready and thank you for doing this. I know that deep down you want this world to be a better place and that you make sacrifices for me. It's time I put my money where my mouth is.*

I'll always protect you and I know you will do the same for me. We'll end this evil monster's reign or die trying.

There was a ting noise from far below metal again metal and Cassandra climbed around to the outside of the tower. It's possible some night security spotted her. She could scale the outside of the tower easily, there's no human alive who could catch her now. She had a few hours to spare and quickly reached the ground. One last grim task and the plan would be in motion. She only hoped Joseph was right. Once again she trusted him with her life but now the risk was greater, she had to trust Anne as well.

* * *

The Newfoundland Vampire   Charles O'Keefe

Cassandra slowly walked beside the Canal Saint-Martin. It was late evening just before midnight, but still lots of people about on a Friday night. Not so many tourists for early November, but with over two million people in the city that made little difference, the swell and hum of blood, thoughts and heartbeats filled her senses. The last time here, well technically not here but Normandy, was horrific, so much blood and death, so many bodies, the stench and of course the Count. In comparison, Paris was so beautiful now, not quiet or clean but still so much better. There was a huge number of cigarette butts on the streets. Unlike Newfoundland and most of North America, almost everyone here still smoked. She was winding her way towards the Crazy Horse bar, it was a strip club but only in the North American perspective. Families went there and fine food and wine was served, she had looked it up earlier on her phone. She wanted some distraction and booze. She also knew it would do fine for the Countess' three victims.

She mulled over what Joseph had said. She couldn't be mad at him for sleeping with Anne, he would probably even mix his blood and body with hers again. He wanted that closeness the blood could provide. She was an interesting person and certainly had sex appeal. What hurt her was that he chose to be with Anne and not her, but she had to move on. Joseph had not called on her for help when he was in danger, had not even told her about the fight with the Countess' goons right away, *he is growing strong and independent, which is what I wanted him to be*. Spending a little time out of Newfoundland was giving her some time to reflect. *Time heals all wounds and perhaps someday we will be back together*. In the meantime, she had a very important decision to make. Joseph had told her of Anne's plan, to kill the Countess and replace her. Cassandra wanted that evil bitch dead too. Even more so now that she had threatened Joseph and his friend. Joseph was her only real family as well, the only descendant left not with any of John in him.

Striking a pre-emptive blow to the Council would be something the Council would never consider. It would be a move that would buy them time, and it would get Anne, and the rest of them, on the inside. One half of the Council only caused death, destruction and misery and the other was too busy preparing to do anything else. Perhaps someday she could be on it and make a better world. She chuckled to herself, for so many years she cared nothing for humanity or the world at all, only concerned with keeping her secret and revenge. Even in the short time she had known Joseph, his hope and compassion for the world was rubbing off on her.

In the corner of her eye was a parent with a small child on a street corner. He held the child up and let him urinate into a drain. Cassandra wrinkled her nose in disgust, not just for the act, but because the child was only six or seven and out much too late.

Heading into the Crazy Horse, she noted the hours on the door and came up with a plan, by three the dancers here would be tired. She would follow three of them, one at a time if needed, and take them. Then it would just be a matter of getting them into a cab and go to the hotel. She would appear to be the helpful friend getting her three drunken friends home. With her telepathy, she could easily disguise her appearance and make the driver forget. One of the interesting differences about France; nudity was completely accepted unlike in North America. It was after two, still teenagers, some tourists, couples, some single men and women made the place half full. Nothing felt perverted or cheap. The place was beautifully decorated with white

linen tablecloths. Cassandra sat near the front. No bouncers
to be seen and no annoying dance music or a deejay.

Paris certainly has class. No doubt Paris has seedy strip
clubs as well, but this certainly wasn't one of them.

Cassandra ordered two bottles of Château Rayas. The
wine was delicious and the pleasant, warm sensation of
intoxication spread up from her toes and all the way to the
top of her head. The cloud it put over her mind helped her
forget what she had to do these innocent women in just a
short time. The show also helped to distract her. It had
eight gorgeous women who sang and danced around the
stage. Each time they left and came back out they had a
little less clothes on until finally they came out nude. The
music was quite good and catchy, performed by an actual
band just off to the side and the women sang in harmony...

You turn me on,
You turn me on,
You turn me in, you turn me out, you turn me round...

Not very original or meaningful lyrics, but it suited their
dancing and the mood of the place. People stood and
clapped, Cassandra did as well. She sat back down and
poured the last of the second bottle in her glass, savoring it.
People started to leave as it was the last show of the night
but she had to wait. The waiter came over and quietly gave
her the check. She laughed it was over eleven-hundred
Euros, an insane amount to pay for two bottles of wine but
what did she care? She'd have that much with her
investments in just over a week. Putting the money in the
booklet and adding another one hundred as a tip, she got
up. Shaking off the drunkenness, she resigned herself for
what was to come next. Making sure to project a different
appearance to anyone who remained, she headed out the
door and around the back. Fortunately for her three

women enjoyed a smoke together. At least it would make this next part quicker.

* * *

The cab rolled down Rue de la Trémoille with Cassandra and her three passengers. Cassandra had made herself to be Julia Roberts in their minds, a simple enough trick. People loved celebrities all over the world and it wasn't hard to get them to go for a drink then drug them. The hotel was right on the corner, blending in almost seamlessly with all the other buildings. The buildings here displayed white and yellow colors with balconies and flowers along many of them, the hotel had blue metal bars along the edges and blue trim around the windows. Three flags from different countries hung outside, one of them British, one Canadian and the last French. It was a nice hotel with old world charm but any enjoyment Cassandra might have gained was over as she knew of what was to come. Giving the driver the cab fare and a generous tip, she completely changed his memory of who was dropped off. *You dropped off four American tourists, three men and a woman, they tipped you and asked you not to mention you saw them.*

Cassandra checked to make sure her sword and daggers remained under her coat, she wasn't planning to use them but she had to be certain. The hotel was expecting her and she was quickly ushered to the elevator and told to go to the top floor. Once again, she made all of the women and herself appear different to everyone else, a necessary precaution no matter what arrangements the Countess had made.

Arriving on the top floor, Cassandra, now carrying one woman on each shoulder and the other in her arms, recognized the same guards she had brought to

Newfoundland. They both turned to her, perhaps noticing her weapons, and pointed to a room. As before, they looked odd wearing smart three-piece suits but brandishing shotguns.

"Please leave your coat and weapons with us. The Countess is unarmed." While he said please the way they both fingered the triggers meant it wasn't a request.

Message received boys, I know the Countess demands obedience. She nodded and removed laid down each woman carefully on the floor, then removed her coat. Placing her weapons on the table and her coat on a hook behind the door.

She retrieved the sleeping women and walked back to the more ornate door, knowing it was where the Countess was and felt one of the guards move behind her. She was nervous, she felt her heart pounding and her throat felt tight. Usually she turned off these human physical traits but she was still in character from the cab just a few moments ago. She had thought over her questions for the Countess and hoped they would give her the answers they needed. She reached out for the Countess' presence and didn't find it. In this unique situation this was a good thing, the ring was on her.

The man opened the door and announced, "Cassandra is here with some unconscious women, should I close the door?"

The Countess was gazing out the window. She was dressed in a white evening gown, and it plunged almost to her behind, revealing her slim back. Her hair was pinned up with a few locks loose and hanging about her neck. She wore nothing on her feet. "Yes Steven, thank you and close the door. Do not disturb us."

These three rooms where joined into one, all tastefully decorated and no doubt expensive. She felt the presence of another guard in the room to one side and another human whose breathing was shallow in the third room.

The Countess turned around and gazed at Cassandra, "They insist on calling you Cassandra, I've stopped arguing. Just pathetic humans after all. You will always be Catherine of Newfoundland to me."

Cassandra knew she would need to stroke her ego to distract her. She laid the three women down once more and curtsied. "Countess, I have the humans you asked for and met with Louis. I drugged the girls and they won't wake for at least a few hours."

The Countess let a smile glance the edge of her mouth, "Yes, thank you for bringing them and for getting here promptly. I'm pleased to see you treat me with respect. I have much influence with the Council and if you continue to prove useful then favors may come your way. Drink?" She held up a wine glass.

Cassandra nodded, "Yes, I'll have a drink, thank you."

The Countess poured them each a glass, "I've spoken with Louis, and he told me of your commitment to the cause. He could not seduce you though, which surprised him more than me. Upset about Joseph mayhap?"

Cassandra kept her emotions firmly shut down, focusing instead on what needed to be done.

She answered as naturally as she could while sipping the wine, "Excellent wine, thank you. I am perturbed but he is young. In time he will come to see that I have a more realistic view of the world. In the meantime I have found pleasure with others."

The Countess moved around and closed both of the doors to the joining rooms. Cassandra took this as a sign that she did not threaten the Countess in the least.

"Sound proof rooms, the guards don't need to know what we say. Do go on, I have not had much contact with others with this ring and I do occasionally enjoy a little pillow talk." The Countess leaned forward, her hands cupped under her chin.

Cassandra was surprised at her openness. Anne's theory about the ring may be correct. *Perhaps one more question though to make certain.* "Yes of course Countess, but first I myself am curious. This ring, I know it shields your presence but does it also cuts you off from telepathic communication? Even with your maker the Count?" Cassandra sat on the plush red velvet couch to the side and the Countess wandered over with the bottle of wine.

Narrowing her eyes at Cassandra for a moment she paused, suspicious but it soon passed and her nonchalant demeanor returned. "You know about the Count and my past, I suppose this little tidbit changes nothing. Yes it does have the drawback of cutting off telepathy. Of course, my guards need no coercion and I received some delightful videos from the Count just recently, so I know he is doing well. The ring also has a strange addictive quality, I find that I do not want to take it off. The sensation of invisibility is like a cool cloak around my shoulders. Why do you ask so many questions?"

Cassandra had prepared for this question, she answered quickly and naturally, "The ring is a thing of magic, something I am not old or lucky enough to have known. I thought perhaps I could hold it, only just for a moment to feel its power."

The Countess laughed, a horrible twisted menacing noise that made Cassandra's skin crawl. Then her voice stiffened, "Do not forget your place Catherine. My generosity has limits. Your compliance has put me in a good mood. The Emperor himself lent me this ring, you're not worthy to lick the soles of his feet. I have served the Council for over three-hundred years. Drink your wine and do not concern yourself further with it."

Cassandra quickly sent a message to Joseph covering it with another gulp of the fine wine. *The ring does cut off all telepathy for the wearer. I consent to the plan fully and will update you when I can. Do not contact me as I must concentrate.* No response came but Cassandra knew Joseph got it, she could sense his presence still in Newfoundland.

"Anne Bonny recently came to Newfoundland and paid me a visit, perhaps you have heard of her?"

As Cassandra studied her face the Countess' eyes opened wide, her face blank, genuinely surprised. She nearly dropped the bottle of wine, just catching it before it hit the floor. It only took a second for her to regain her composure. "Anne Bonny, I haven't heard that name for some time. The Council is aware of her, of course, but she is reclusive, out of contact with any vampires for a good century now, fascinating. She no doubt shed some light on John, among other matters."

Cassandra knew this nasty business would be worth it. The Countess would not be able to resist becoming the first member of the Council to contact the reclusive Anne.

"Anne is a good fighter, sexy, and much like yourself, interested in both men and women. She…" Cassandra paused for just a moment, letting a little emotion come into her voice, "bested me in combat and then later seduced me. She went down on me with great skill, bringing me to a much greater climax that Joseph or any man could. We had sex together then with humans, an orgy similar to the one you walked in in the sixties. Later she had sex with Joseph as well, no doubt satisfying his need for sex and blood."

The Countess began to loosen the clothes of the women lying on the floor, preparing them so she could feast. "Anne perhaps told you that her creator, John Roberts, wanted her to join the Council many years ago. She refused and they fought viciously. Perhaps a visit to Anne would be fortuitous. I could do what Black Bart failed to do. She must learn her place."

Cassandra quickly signaled to Joseph, *She is coming with at least three guards, I'll let you know the moment we depart.* To the Countess she replied, "A good idea, I did not appreciate her seeing Joseph behind my back and would like put her in line as well." This last part had just a sliver of truth.

Finishing her glass of wine, the Countess topped up the glass and motioned to the women. "Then it's settled. Once I'm done with these three we'll depart. I was going to give Joseph instructions anyway, young or not he can create others that we will subjugate. Speaking of, bring these women to the point of death. As you do it I will turn each one into a slave for the cause. When the time comes they will serve."

Cassandra knew these women would be turned but did not anticipate helping so much, it disgusted her but she knew to convince the Countess she would have to relish in the task. Cassandra finished her wine and gulped, steeling herself, "One last question Countess, why don't I just turn them completely?"

The Countess sighed as she pulled down the straps of her dress, revealing her naked body to Cassandra once more. "Since you and Joseph have already dealt with one, I see no harm in explaining this part. If you recall, you fought a thrall in New Orleans. He acted like Donald but of course was not him. He was a thrall, a brain-washed vampire in a sense. Someone who can be programmed and will carry out any commands given to them. The technique of creating one was taught to me by the Count, who was shown it by the Emperor himself. None of that matters though, the mission is need to know. All you need to know is to follow my instructions, if you know what's good for you."

Cassandra saw that the time for discussion had ended. Cassandra tore into one of the women. Just innocent humans and she was disgusted by what the Countess had made her do. As the blood covered her face, cheeks and chest, she hated the Countess with every fiber of her being. Blood spurted from their necks, covering their clothes, the wall and even the ceiling. Cassandra was forced to gorge herself on the blood and felt their fear and desperation as she continued to drain these women. What bothered her even more than the act of bringing them near death was that a small part of was enjoying it. It was becoming clear to her that she needed someone to be a positive influence in her life, someone to help her be a better person. People like the Countess only brought out the worst in her. They had to kill the Countess, or die in the attempt . . . they had to.

She finished the grizzly task of draining all three women and wiped the blood out of her eyes. She felt she might puke, he was so full of blood. She took the dark towel offered to her by the Countess and stood up. The Countess beamed with pleasure and Cassandra found herself unable to turn away as the Countess turned these innocent women into thralls. Cassandra waited for process to end, and the Countess' final hours to begin.

Chapter 15: The French Connection

Joseph lay in bed, faced turned to the window. He was exhausted, nervous, excited and terrified. He had just received word from Cassandra, the Countess and her guards had departed for St. Pierre. He had planned for this and enjoyed the blood of two moose the night before and the pleasure of sex and a blood embrace with Anne. He felt the plan was solid, necessary, but still dangerous and by no means guaranteed to succeed. *What if the Countess was lying about the ring? Could she contact the Count? Would the Count know the instant of her death? Could Anne successfully impersonate the Countess for long enough to help us? What would Shatner and the other decent members make of this? So many damn questions and no good answers.* He was pleased that before everything started with Anne, he got a lot of course work done at Memorial. He could take the next week off if need be. He had doubts about his own fighting prowess and had concerns on how well the three of them would fight as a team. The men, the Countesses' bodyguards, weighed on his mind as well. Sure they worked for the Countess and the Council, but he didn't want to kill them. He hoped that somehow it wouldn't be necessary. He had plenty of fights with vampires under his belt: John Snow in Bowring Park, Donald in that abandoned building on Bennett Avenue, Marlon and Scarlett just a few nights ago at Topsail Beach, all of them sudden, and no chance to prepare. He hoped that planning would make the difference this time. Joseph reminded himself that the odds looked better than before, three vampires versus one and her guards. This time Anne had explained the plan and he had to say it was a good one.

She resembled the Countess more every day and her ability to anticipate her actions should come in handy tonight. He wouldn't be able to get back to sleep now, his mind was racing. Cassandra had told him she would be in St. Pierre around nine tonight. It would be a short flight but first they had to prepare. He had already come up with the lie to tell his parents. Recently he had wanted to have a geeky weekend with friends, he had planned to play board games and Dungeons and Dragons all weekend, and it could be certainly could be now. The sun was completely up and his headache and tiredness in full force, it didn't matter though. With his heart pounding and his stomach churning he had to get up.

He contacted Anne, *I'll be over to get you soon. Cassandra and the Countess have left Paris and will be there by nine.* Anne was now staying at Ocean Quest, a spa and small hotel just a few kilometers away, close enough for them to talk telepathically.

The reply came quickly, *I'll be ready Joe, remember your weapons and I dearly hope Cassandra is right in her assessment of the Countess.*

Joseph shivered at the thought of having to be around the Countess again. He hoped it would be for the last time. There was an important detail with the fight, they couldn't kill the Countess outright, and the three of them had to force her into an embrace to get all her memories for Anne. He would have to know everything about her, every last sordid memory and detail. He sighed and his shoulders sank. *This will be the hardest thing I have ever done.*

His parents would be up soon and he would have to push all these emotions down, something unfortunately he was becoming more skilled at than he would like. He had already lied about all the sleeping and his paler than usual complexion. He had stayed home with his parents the past few days, with Anne and the Council he wanted to keep an eye on them. He got out of bed, took his sword and daggers, retrieved a gun from the old horse shed, and put them all in the Sonata before his parents got up. He remembered the two suits of body armor he had stuck in the old well house and got them too, if the Countess guards fought for her, they might come in handy. He spent some time with Jude and Ginger.

His mom came out down the stairs, "Good morning Joe, you're on the go early today."

He forced a smile and said, "I didn't want to sleep the day away, managed to get off the internet earlier last night and get busy. I have plans for tonight and tomorrow."

His mom came forward and gave him a hug, "Of course dear, did I tell you we missed you and we love you very much?"

He gave her a quick kiss and hugged her back. "Yes you did, I missed you both too."

His Dad came down the stairs and said, "Good morning Joseph."

"Good morning Dad" he replied, smiling. Joseph continued with his mom, "Sara and Terry invited people up to their cabin in Brigus Junction, I'm going to go into Memorial to do some research before I go."

His mom focused on him, "Are you sure you're eating right with this vegetarian diet? You look pale."

He would have to come up with a solution for the paleness, for now another lie would have to do. "I'm fine, okay?"

She relented, "All right, Have a good night and be careful."

"I'll be careful. I'll see you Sunday night." Before his façade faded he grabbed his coat and headed out the door. He reached out and felt Anne's presence nearby, not warm and calming like Cassandra's but still friendly to him and charged with anticipation. She must have sensed him as well and sent him the message, *good you're on your way. I'm here as Beth. The plane is at the airport and ready to fly. See you thusly.*

He chuckled a little and said, "Thusly, I like it. Not something you hear every day."

Even though he would face the Countess with Cassandra and Anne, he didn't have anyone now to reassure him. Cassandra was someone he had trusted before, someone he knew would protect him in a fight, help him prepare, but he didn't know what Anne would do or say. The pressure on his shoulders now felt immense. Maybe this is what he needed, to face a difficult decision and understand what his immortality would keep costing him. He could not help but consider the vampire council, both sides. Even though he hated everything the Countess and Count stood for he had fought with their blessing. This time, if discovered, the Count and others would try to kill them, and it could even speed up whatever huge attack they had in the works. The good side of the Council, well Joseph didn't believe they would kill any of them, but they could be mad. He sighed and flicked through songs on his iPhone.

At the end of Cherry Lane the light was red and he settled on "Outta my head" by Fastball...

Sometimes I feel like I am drunk behind the wheel, the wheel of possibilities

Joseph felt that the weight of many choices he could make and knew lots of different ways this could turn out but he just couldn't figure all the variables. What he would say to Cassandra when he saw her again? *Will this end my relationship with Cassandra forever, or is this some kind of new beginning?*

Before he could consider the question he pulled into the parking lot of Ocean Quest. Full of nervous energy he quickly headed to the front desk, his phone in his pocket ready to dispose of it. A woman he knew from doing deliveries was at the front desk, Melanie, and she smiled at him.

"Joseph! How are you? Have a delivery for us?"

Joseph smiled, he liked Melanie, she was upbeat and friendly. "No I'm actually here to see someone. Can you tell what room Beth's in?"

Melanie smiled and playfully punched his shoulder. "Good for you! Beth's a hottie, very exotic and her accent is awesome. You have fun tonight, she's in room 203 just up the stairs."

"Yeah she is kind of hot and I do like her accent. Well it was nice seeing you."

Melanie smiled as she answered the phone. "Good afternoon Ocean Quest Spa, how may I help you?" she waved to Joseph. He started to head upstairs to get Anne, when he heard a thump outside. He continued to the top of the stairs and turned to the window, Anne got up from all fours and headed toward his car. He sighed, *well I guess she's ready to go*. He went outside to the car.

"You could have told me you planned to jump out the window." He tapped his fingers against his leg, staring at Anne.

Anne pushed her hair out of her face and laughed. "Now what fun would that be? How about opening the boot lad, I don't imagine you want me to break the lock."

Joseph felt a shiver run up his spine and his hairs stand on end. The car keys hung loose in his hand. Anne resembled the Countess a lot now. She hadn't used the accent, but her hair was no longer red, her freckles gone and her cheekbones now the high arched kind. She wasn't a dead ringer but she could certainly pass for a sister or other close relative. He had only seen her last night and the facial changes blew his mind.

She took the keys from him and quickly opened the trunk. She also took Joseph's phone and wrapped it up in her clothes several times, enough to muffle what the bug would pick up. "Not bad for one night huh? Now get in the car please, time's a wasting."

Joseph snapped out of the trance and got in the car, forgetting to hold the door open for Anne. As they drove he said, "That's amazing. Your hair and skin had changed last night but how did you change your face so fast? Cassandra said changing our appearance took many nights, I assumed she meant weeks or even months."

Anne turned off the music and put on her seatbelt. "Thanks for agreeing to this, I know this is a huge risk but it has to happen, we have to try. As for my transformation, our physical skills get better as we practice them. I stayed up all night after I saw you and I have had almost three centuries of practice changing my facial features. It help to pass the time on my private island and I suspected one day it would come in handy."

Joseph glanced over at her, looking into her lovely blue-green eyes. "I just never thought about anyone wanting to change their appearance quickly. I thought we would only need to do it every seventy or eighty years but I see now it could be more often. A few details about tonight have me wondering."

Anne arched her eyebrow and tilted her head but gave no reply, *if she's nervous she is sure doing a great job of covering it up*.

Anne looked out the window for a long moment then turned back to him, "Do go on Joseph, I would like a little distraction before tonight. I may have missed some detail but I hope thar not be the case."

As Joseph drove, the fog wrapped around them like a blanket, it came at them in waves. Even though it was broad daylight he had to slow down. He hoped the plane was already here and it could take off. He fought against his daytime headache and aching limbs. Briefly rubbing his eyes he focused on the road once more. "If you become the Countess, then Anne is dead to the world, including other vampires. So…umm I know this is crass, but what happens to all your money and assets?"

Anne laughed, "You sure know how to sweet talk a girl, don't you?"

Joseph flushed, regretting what he said, but Anne gently squeezed his hand and continued. "Not to worry lad, I have it all looked after. In fact I've arranged it so that if I can't reclaim my identity in a few years you will both have it all. You'll be quite a wealthy man, if that is important to you."

Joseph was left speechless for a moment. "I…well…I don't know what to say."

"Just say thank you and keep us on the road."

Joseph had wandered a little into the other lane, he quickly corrected the car. "Well thank you Anne, I guess the last detail I'm concerned about is the guards. While they're human, they're trained to kill vampires. Have you thought of some way to incapacitate them?"

Anne smiled and laid a hand on his knee, "You're welcome, I want you both to be happy. Yes I have thought of the men. I have a flash-bang and a smoke grenade that will incapacitate them and hopefully affect the Countess as well. Remember, we all need to link with her so she has to be alive for a few minutes at the end."

Joseph nodded and took the exit for the airport. The fog was even thicker out here but he supposed with a private plane Anne could make them take off, or perhaps even pilot the plane herself. *There's still so much I don't know about her but I do like her attention to details and this fight is well thought out.* "That is a good plan, I will send Cassandra a mental warning as soon as she gets in the door to leap out of the way. We'll just need to board up any windows, I saw on a show that those kinds of grenades will shatter glass."

This time Anne nodded and Joseph turned his eyes back to the road as they made it to the airport and into the long-term parking lot. Joseph turned off the car and got out. This time he remembered to open Anne's door and pop the trunk. He left his phone in the trunk, the Council could track its movement to St. Pierre after all. A man showed up as they approached the building and took their bags and Joseph's keys. Anne slipped him some money, and said "Thank you."

The man smiled at Anne, "*Soyez les bienvenus.*"

Joseph whispered to Anne as they walked, "Thank you for arranging all this, I see now it's the right move. Hopefully we can get some sleep on the plane."

She kissed him lightly on the cheek, "You're welcome laddie. This will be hard but you're stronger than you know. The flight normally takes only an hour and a half, but I've asked him to slow it down to three hours. We'll still be there in plenty of time."

Joseph nodded and settled back in his chair. He had to admit it was nice back on a private plane, this one didn't have the size and splendor of the Council's jet but the seats felt soft and comfortable. He relaxed, pleased at the lack of a flight attendant, he would rather be alone with his thoughts for a while.

* * *

Joseph was startled awake as the plane landed. "Wha . . . where am I?" he shook his head and cleared it. *Right, about to have another bloody confrontation with a vampire, what else is new!* He was sweating and his heart pounded in his chest, he took several deep breaths, trying to calm himself.

The Newfoundland Vampire   Charles O'Keefe

Anne was more at ease and yawned and stretched as the plane came to a stop. She glared at Joseph but said nothing, she didn't have to. *I have to do this, it's not just my life but Anne and Cassandra's too, maybe even my friends and family all depend on it. Have to get my shit together.* He took a big gulp of water and focused, *I can do this, I'm not alone and I've learned, combat is almost become normal for me.*

Anne collected up her gear and strode out of the plane. Joseph followed and as they got in a purple caravan that drove off in the bright early afternoon sun. He always found it interesting that back in St. John's it was pea soup fog but, here it was sunny and clear, even warm. St. Pierre was a part of France even thought it was just twenty kilometers away from Newfoundland, he loved that fact, it made Newfoundland different from anywhere else in Canada. He watched the houses go by as they drove to an abandoned building just across the harbor from the ferry terminal.

Several horses stood in people's yards, at least one other just tied on near a wooden walkway. He liked St. Pierre, had just last summer visited there with his parents. It was quiet and people enjoyed a simpler way of life, everyone even had two hour lunches. They approached a building he remembered from his previous visit. The taxi driver had told them it was the old airport hangar. The windows and doors boarded up and an old power boat was up on blocks behind it, its seaworthy days long gone. Some houses lay around the building but not many. *This is a perfect spot, if we play music loud during the fight no one may even suspect anything.*

As if she read his mind, Anne answered, "Don't worry about the neighbors. They think a loud party is happening here tonight. I brought you a gas mask as I know you have trouble with smoke."

"Good and thanks, it is hard to just stop breathing. So do you want to train...er, practice before they get here?"

"No more training do you require. I set up some cots inside and I'll take another nap. We still have about seven hours before they get here. Check the place out of if you want."

Joseph couldn't help but laugh a little, he recognized the line from *Return of the Jedi*. Anne produced a crowbar and began to pull off the boards on the door, Joseph quickly moved up to help her. Without his vampire strength it was not easy but after a minute or two they managed. "Star Wars! You quoted Star Wars, did you see those movies?" He was smiling, he always loved it when someone make a geeky reference.

Anne tossed the crowbar to the ground and lay back in a military style cot that was big enough for two, smiling mischievously. "I actually quoted from Return of the Jedi, get your movies right laddie. What do you think you're the only vampire who likes science fiction? I did just lie on beach for almost a century, I've seen more movies that you will in the next twenty years. So yeah of course I've seen the original trilogy, don't get me started on those piece of crap prequels though."

Joseph was genuinely surprised, this was a different side of Anne. "No I didn't think...I'm just...well"

She motioned with her fingers for him to come over, he obliged and sat on the cot with her. She reached out and took his hand in hers, she was full of blood and her hand was warm and soft.

She looked into his eyes and smiled. "Surprised? I can manage it sometimes. I get it you know, the world has changed. Geeky movies have taken over and who am I to argue? Oh and to answer your next question yes I heard about episode VII, well to be honest I plucked it from your mind just then."

Joseph frowned for a second but wasn't mad, it certainly wasn't a dark secret. Besides he was much more distracted by the fact that Anne let go of his hand and pulled off her shirt.

"Oh...umm what're you doing? I thought you wanted to…"

She held a finger up to his lips. "You have your watch correct? Well set it to go off in four hours. Push those metal barrels against the door. They would make plenty of racket to wake both of us. I could die tonight, you might too. If that's the case I want to be shagged good and proper one last time, I'm sure it will help us both relax." She quickly had her pants off, revealing her slim and toned body. "Hell, twice, if you're up to the occasion."

Joseph found that, as usual, arguing with a half-naked woman was a waste of time. It would be a great release and she could be right. If this was his last night, he would like to get laid one more time. Quickly trying to drag a heavy, old black oil barrel across the room and undressing at the same time proved tricky and he fell. They both laughed as he got up and pushed the barrel in place. With his massive hard on, he stumbled over to her.

She smiled and flicked him down on the bed, practically tearing his clothes off. "This time I'm taking you for a ride. Let's see how well you do without your vampire stamina. I still want you to still bite, I don't care where, just let the blood flow when you cum."

Joseph reached behind her and unclasped her bra. She then lifted up so he could pull off her underwear. In a blink she had his underwear off and her wet warmness enveloped him. *Mmm, yeah Anne, that's it.* He reached up and cupped her firm breasts, squeezing the nipples as she moved up and down on him. *I won't last long but I can hopefully get hard again shortly after.*

* * *

The time had come. Joseph had spent the last few hours checking out every nook and cranny of the building and practicing some martial arts. Anne spent it mediating in the middle of the floor. He felt Cassandra's presence draw near, she had landed at the airport and would be here in moments. They had arranged the barrels in a circle around the door, it would both intensify the blast from the flash-bang grenades and give Cassandra some cover. Anne also had a smoke grenade to add to the confusion and would make it harder for them to shoot with any accuracy. They had also tied a strong rope to the door, Joseph would use it to quickly pull it shut and bar the entrance as soon as they got inside.

His heart pounded in his chest and his hands sweated. He had his gun in the back of his pants, a silver dagger tucked in one pocket, two wooden ones in the back pockets, his sword strapped to his side and a smoke canister on his belt. *I'm a walking arsenal! At least I'm ready for this.*

Anne shifted back and forth on the balls of her feet, her sword in her hand and her dagger in a belt sheath. He was nervous and blurted out, "What about the music? When will it come on?"

"Joseph focus!" She growled at him. "There with is a timer on it, remember the plan. You take out the guards and get the Countess into the fight with us. We fight to wound her, not kill. We have to make her bleed, make her weak. The guards will have Cassandra's weapons, help her get them back. I can handle the Countess for a bit."

Joseph nodded and wiped his hands in his pants. "Before we start I want you to know I love you."

Anne grinned and turned to face him, "I know."

She is perfect at breaking tension, even in a moment like this. He laughed a little, *another Star Wars reference, good one Anne.* They both wore the body armor he had brought with him. The gas mask lay at his feet in a box. His senses on edge, every rotten board creaked and the sound dug into his ears like nails. The crunching of something heavy on gravel let him know of a car coming and his focus returned. He gripped the rope with one hand, the other hand he put his finger through the ring of the grenade pin. He hid just to left of the door while Anne stood a good thirty feet outside the ring of barrels.

Cassandra entered his mind, *the taller guard has my weapons in a case. The Countess has her rapiers but does not suspect an attack. Remember no matter what happens or what we have to do I will always love you, my beloved. Don't think harshly of me, in time you'll understand I always did what needed to be done.*

Joseph quickly replied, *I...love you too...I am starting to accept what this life makes us do and while I don't agree with it...I do understand a little more. As soon as the door closes jump behind the barrels, we have a surprise planned.* Joseph found then as with many combats while the fighting happened very quickly for him time slowed down.

The Countess entered the building. He smiled when he saw the Countess' face, her eyes wide and her mouth slack for a split second. The stereo snapped to life.

I love you, Pumpkin.

I love you, Hunny Bunny.

"Anne, what the bloody hell is going on here? What kind of dump have you brought me to and why..." Whatever the Countess might have said was drowned out.

The guards entered, with Cassandra in front of him. Joseph pulled the rope hard and the door slammed shut. A small part of Joseph's mind registered what was playing, it was the soundtrack to *Pulp Fiction*, one of his favorite movies.

Everybody be cool this is a robbery!

Any of you fuckin' pricks move and I'll execute every motherfucking last one of you!

Cassandra shoved the guards aside and jumped behind the barrels. Joseph pulled the pin and tossed the grenade at them, Anne did the same. He ducked behind the barrel, put on the gas mask and closed his eyes. The Countess' eyes opened wide and one guard jumped in front of her, his back turned to Joseph and Anne. There was an explosion of lights and huge boom that hit Joseph in the chest and along with a hundred *ting* sounds as rubber balls bounced off of the barrels. Two of guards screamed in pain, there was also two thumps.

The guards slammed backwards into the barrels, dazed and insensate. The Countess held her ears, possibly deafened. The guards lay on the floor, plainly hurt and Joseph smelled their blood as it ran out onto the cracked floorboards. The noise and the force from the blast was incredible, plus the blinding flash of light.

To make the situation more bizarre, an instrumental surfing song started and the fight was on. Two of the men remained still, but the others did their best to move into action. The Countess had her swords in hand and launched herself at Anne, she fought like a woman possessed. Anne bared her fangs and the Countess' eyes flared red like the fires of hell. The Countess forward motions and jumps pushed Anne towards the back of the room. It was an incredible scene as the two vampires who resembled each other so much squared off.

Joseph rolled the smoke canister at the men, further hampering any chance they had of shooting straight. Cassandra was on her hands and knees behind a barrel. She quickly found the case her sword was in and held it out. Joseph drew his sword and brought the hilt down on the lock, smashing it open. He got the weapons to Cassandra and she nodded. Her eyes bloodshot as tears ran out of them.

Handle the guards, I'll help Anne. You're strong dear one and ready.

Ready as I'll ever be, he sent back, *I'll take care of them.*

Joseph stood and helped Cassandra towards Anne and the Countess, he knew she could fight fine without her eyes once the distance was gone. To his dismay the door had swung back open, the hinges possibly ruined by the grenade, any advantage that the smoke would give wouldn't last long. Turning his attention to Anne and the Countess, he could hardly fathom the sight. It reminded him of when Cassandra fought John back in Newfoundland. Clothes, steel and flesh became almost a blur, even with vampire sight he could barely make it out. The Countess leaped, twirled and spun through the air, stabbing, slashing, parrying and thrusting. Occasionally she found her mark, the body armor helped, but blood had already started to run down Anne's legs, she had a large gash on her cheek. The Countess was not without marks, Anne's sword and dagger had sliced her dress almost to shreds, and blood ran down her left leg and her right arm. Both of them used silver weapons and the wounds did not heal quickly. They growled and yelled at each other. It was a savage display of hatred and violence. A thought occurred to Joseph that it was dance or sorts, they both moved to the beat of the music that blared through the speakers. Anne showed the extent of her martial arts training, spin kicks, uppercuts with both weapons, roundhouse kicks and front kicks to push her back. Anne did a somersault and landed behind the Countess, slashing viciously at her back, carving her flesh and making her dress fall completely away.

Cassandra was perhaps unsure where to join in the fray for a few seconds, she sent to Joseph, *tell me what you see, my vision is still blurry.*

Joseph glanced for a second longer, *amazing, incredible fighters with over four-hundred years of training between them, but we must not just stand by. Anne stands by herself for a second while the Countess recovers from a gash on her back.*

Yes of course, I am ready to engage, deal with the guards, they cannot escape, do what must be done.

Joseph nodded and turned back just as the Countess delivered a vicious knee to Anne's head, causing her to stagger for a second and most likely breaking her nose. The guards began to move. One coughed and wheezed with the smoke, waving his hands and trying to clear it. The other was clever and kicked the smoke canister out the door. Joseph couldn't talk with them, couldn't even yell, the best he could do was raise his sword protectively and project his thoughts, *Put down your weapons and surrender. The Countess is about to die, you no longer need to serve her.* The coughing guard moved towards the door and Joseph knew he had to act. Running forward he quickly closed the distance. The guard had reached the door and Joseph shoved him back as hard as he could, despite the man's weight he went flying back and slammed into a barrel, collapsing to the floor. Joseph had never hit a human so hard but he saw no other choice, he couldn't let the man escape, he knew the truth of what they had done.

The other guard leveled the shotgun at Joseph and fired, the wooden pellets slammed him in the chest and put him down on his back. It hurt like hell. The wind was knocked out of him and for a second Joseph couldn't breathe, before he remembered he didn't have to. His breathing stopped and his fangs descended. If these assholes wanted to die for the Countess he would have to oblige. Joseph was certain that without the body armor he would be dead. He rolled and got up, weaving from side to side as he had seen in the movies. The guard unloaded the second barrel of the shotgun at him but missed. Joseph closed the distanced and slashed with his sword, the blade came down and cut the man almost completely in two. Joseph's face was covered in blood and his stomach wanted to lurch with the horrendous sight. He turned his head to gage how Cassandra and Anne fared against the Countess.

The fight continued but clearly Anne and Cassandra would win. The Countess was tiring and blood ran from her arms, legs, chest and back in torrents. Cassandra was bleeding from both arms and legs but fought with all the strength and skill she had. Anne had a large welt that sealed one eye shut and her left arm lay limp at her side, perhaps broken. The Countess still refused to give up and lunged at Anne but Cassandra was there to stop the strike that may have taken her head off. Turning back he saw more problems. Another guard stood up and raised a gun towards him, the man next to the barrel did not stir while the third remaining guard only twitched on the floor. Ducking as he saw the man pull the trigger, the bullet ran along the top of his head. Blood and hair flew off and Joseph gritted his teeth with the pain.

Retrieving his own gun from the back of his pants he emptied the clip, "I'll kill you you Goddamned bastard!" He screamed at the top of his lungs, he felt his eyes burn and knew they had turned red, the gas mask he had worn fell to the floor with a strap gone. He wasn't the best shot but with a whole clip he managed to hit the man in both arms and one leg. He fell to the ground and a shot went off into the ceiling. Joseph charged forward, dropping the gun and getting his sword. He reached up with a hand and pulled off the gas mask. He used the back of his hand to wipe away the blood that ran down into his eyes. He leaped on top of the guard just as the man tried to shoot him point blank in the face. Joseph grabbed the guard's hand and crushed it. The man's mouth opened wide and spit flew from it, he howled in pain but Joseph was too enraged to care. He stabbed the man through the chest and pinned him to the floor. Blood poured out of his mouth and his hands fell to the ground. Joseph felt a jolt of incredible pain as another guard, quickly recovered it seemed, stabbed him in the side of his throat with a dagger.

Unable to scream, he opened his mouth in silent furry. Turning with raw instinct and hatred, he slashed viciously with his open hand, his sword stuck in the floor. The move caught the guard completely by surprise. Joseph's hand connected with the guards' skull and smashed bone into his brain. The guard collapsed to the ground, his eyes open but unseeing.

He had lost focus on the music, the other fight, and everything else around him, only pain and survival mattered. Carefully pulling the dagger out of his throat, Joseph wrapped the wound tight with cloth he tore from his own pants leg. He saw the final guard try to crawl out the door and he knew he could not let him escape. He knew this night would haunt him forever but it was too late. Grabbing a discarded shotgun he got in front of the guard, tears streamed down Joseph's face and the final guard mouthed the words "Please Don't!" Joseph hit him with as little force as he could with the butt of the gun. It knocked him out cold but thankfully not dead. Joseph finally turned back to the all-female vampire encounter.

The Countess was drenched in blood, missing her left arm and part of her jaw. Anne had one eye swollen shut and the other hung loosely on her cheek, blood oozing from all over her. Cassandra was also coated in blood and her arms held at her stomach. Joseph didn't want to know what she was holding in. Anne had the Countess down on her knees with her one arm behind her back. Anne's other hand was clenched tightly over her throat. Anne mentally screamed at him, *get over here now! We must finish this. Do it before all her blood is gone!*

Cassandra turned to him, her eyes red and filled with tears. She echoed the thoughts albeit a little less harshly, *we have all come too far not to finish this. To strike this blow against evil we all must know her fully. Let us end it, beloved.*

Joseph didn't bother to reply, letting the shotgun fall to the floor he walked over to them. The Countess eyes burned with hatred and defiance, they tried to burrow into Joseph's skull. They plunged her fangs into her beaten body and she bellowed with pain and frustration. "The Count will avenge me and you all will die! The world belongs to us and you have made the greatest mistake of your pathetic live…" the last word turned into a blood curdling howl, a death scream that chilled Joseph to his very soul. What came next was worse, the thousands she had killed, the children, the blood, the torture, the hideous laughter of her and the Count. The most disturbing part for Joseph was the life draining from so many eyes. The thousands of people the Countess had killed she had stared almost every one of them in the eyes the moment their souls left their bodies, leaving just dead pieces of flesh.

* * *

Mercifully, the embrace took a minute although it had felt like hours. When it ended, Joseph discovered that there was another way for vampires to die; the complete loss of blood. Her body felt like a dried up husk in his hands and he dropped it in disgust and vomited loudly. In the moment he finished vomiting he saw the body turn to ash on the wooden planks. As Joseph expected, Anne put on the ring and her presence immediately vanished. Joseph was thankful at least enough remained of his windpipe and throat to puke. Anne and Cassandra looked terribly wounded and needed blood. Cassandra very carefully put Anne's eye back in the socket and then dragged the unconscious guard over to her. Anne and Cassandra tore and the man's clothes and sank their fangs into arteries. Joseph didn't have the energy or the courage to stop them and closed his eyes. The music ended and the slurping gave him the dry heaves, his stomach was thankfully empty.

With incredible effort, Anne stood and spoke. "I'll never be able to repay you two for what you have done here and I would rather we never spoke of it again. I will have a cleanup crew take care of the bodies. The story for the Council, if needed, will be simple. Anne attacked me and it was only with the help of Cassandra and Joseph that I survived. You two will look like heroes and be left alone. For tonight though, we must rest. I have a house rented for us nearby, I trust, Joseph, you can manage to drive us there."

Joseph nodded and pointed to this throat. Cassandra made sure the bandage was on tight and kissed his forehead, looking deep into his eyes with tears in hers. He reached up and wiped away her tears. Joseph retrieved his sword and gun. Cassandra smiled at him through her tears. She whispered in his mind, *my beloved, so strong. I will be here when you want to talk about this and I hope you will be for me too. We did a good thing tonight and evil was dealt just the first of many fatal blows.*

Part 3:

The past came back to haunt him

Chapter 16: What about now?

Joseph pulled into the only free spot he could find on Duckworth Street. It was almost three blocks from where he had to drop off an order. It had snowed almost non-stop for a month now, February usually sucked in Newfoundland. The snow was a good three feet high in spots and some businesses almost had tunnels going to the doors rather than walkways. He wouldn't normally be doing deliveries but he was covering for the delivery driver. He only came in on Saturdays and Thursday nights, when it wasn't busy and the other staff didn't want to work. Today and for the rest of the week a staff member was away on a snowmobile trip. He still hated to be up during the day and out around on such a cold, miserable day but appearances had to be kept up and it was good for him to be busy.

Joseph didn't enjoy the last few months at all. That night in St. Pierre still haunted him. He started waking up in the night yelling, losing interest in his hobbies and never smiled or laughed anymore. It had gotten to the point where he even had went to a counselor. At first, the counselor made him feel even worse, he couldn't tell her that he had killed three people and let another die. He knew how it worked, it was supposed to be in confidence but if someone admitted to a death, it would be reported to the police.

Eventually, though, talking with the counselor did help. He talked about Cassandra, Anne and even Roxanne, without all the details. He expressed how he was lonely and that while he enjoyed sex he wanted more, he wanted a real connection. The counselor helped him accept that he couldn't try to change Cassandra. She made him see that he was a strong person and didn't need to worry about her changing him. After a month of talking, he knew she was right, he did need Cassandra in his life and she deserved another chance.

By the end of December, he began talking with Cassandra about that night, she was the only one he could talk to about everything. He remembered what she told him the first night they talked after the fight, "We have to trust that Anne's deception is working. Neither of us have heard from the Council. You have to accept that what we did was for the greater good, those men died in the service of evil. I am immensely proud of you for doing what needed to be done. You understand what it takes to save this world. "

Joseph told her everything about what had happened with Anne and Roxanne. Cassandra shared what happened in Paris, the orgy with Anne and how she had nearly killed the pedophile in Florida back in October. After all the horrors he had known from the Countess' memories, he was only mildly shocked at how far the punishment had gone. Joseph thought about the crimes he had committed and maybe that was better justice then the police could give. By New Year's Eve, Cassandra had agreed to meet his parents and by the end of January, the counseling stopped. He and Cassandra had starting having sex and sharing their blood again, it was a comfort and release for him. She was starting to take an interest in his hobbies, they could still train with swords and he could teach her some martial arts. Joseph discovered that she loved to take long walks in the woods and they often went together. She was also learning how to paint and Joseph encouraged her and even went along to a few classes. They went on dates and he learned more about Newfoundland history than he ever had before. Perhaps above it all though they had come to an agreement, they could stop criminals without anyone getting killed. Life with Cassandra was always interesting, he had come to enjoy it and was excited to see what would happen next.

The Newfoundland Vampire   Charles O'Keefe

He had managed to finish his degree, deferment of his exams with a note from his counselor had helped immensely, and by the end of February he was starting to be more like his old self. He had settled into a routine of ten to fifteen hours at the business and the rest of the time tending to his dad's marina. His parents soon left for Florida again, this time staying for the rest of winter. His dad wanted Joseph to learn all the ins and outs of handling the Marina before they left. Joseph continued to play poker at bars, he only used his telepathy some of the time and felt he had gotten better. He kept about half his winnings to invest and the other half went to charity. He also enjoyed playing poker online.

The snow crunched under his feet, it was bitter minus fifteen degrees today and with no powers, he felt it. He managed put his ear buds in and pull his hat down as far as it would go. As usual, he put on music to help him focus and not dwell so much on the past. Robbie Robertson's words made a lot of sense...

What about now? Forget about tomorrow, it's too far away.

He would focus on the now. He was immortal, powerful and had most of his friends and family around him, plus of course Cassandra. She had helped him deal with everything and made him laugh. He continued to walk down the street with his box under one arm. He tried not to be upset that it had started to snow again, the start of what could possibly be the third snowstorm this week.

* * *

"Fuck!" Green was pissed off as he walked out of the courthouse on Duckworth Street. While his hand and knees had healed from the attack last October, on a cold day like today, they stung like a bitch. His lawyer, a long-haired man whose name he couldn't even remember, put a hand on his shoulder. "Keep your spirits up Mr. Green, the case has another week yet and we haven't brought out our character witnesses…"

Green tuned out the rest of what his lawyer said. Green knew he was going to lose the case and go to jail. *Lousy shit-eating bastards! The worst part was sober for court. That sure as hell won't be the case to…*

He spotted a car parked a little down the street, a gold Hyundai and something tugged at his mind. He rubbed his aching hand as his moron lawyer continued to spout off more nonsense about his case.

Green just nodded, eventually the lawyer waved goodbye and wandered off. Green squinted and then opened his eyes wide. *The car, let me check my e-mail.* He quickly went through Phil's messages and found it, *the turd drove a gold Hyundai Sonata and it was parked on Duckworth Street a bit after lunch.*

He pumped his fist in triumph and said out loud, "Finally! I got this lousy douchebag." Scanning up and down the street as the snow started to swirl he couldn't spot him. He went up to the car and took a picture of the license plate. *I've got people who will help, now isn't the time or the place. I'll find where he lives and get him when he doesn't expect it.*

A car went by and drenched him in slush and snow. He gave the asshole the finger then spit on the Hyundai, and dumped his coffee on the windshield. *I'll get my revenge, with any luck his girlfriend will be around too.* Smiling to himself, he headed back to his place, trudging through the accumulating snow. Soon it would be time for some coke; today he finally had a reason to celebrate.

Chapter 17: The Montreal Meeting

Joseph woke up Friday afternoon, the sun was up but it was hard to tell. Snow was still coming down, it started yesterday afternoon and was only now starting to let up. His headache and tiredness was there but the house was too full of noise for him to sleep any longer. In particular, his mom was knocking on the door, "Joseph it's past 2:30! It's not healthy for you to sleep anymore." She came in his room and sat on his bed, "Your sleep schedule will be all out of whack if you keep this up. What kept you up so late?"

He rubbed his eyes and thought again, remembering that last night ended up as a six hour poker session. Normally he didn't bother with tournaments but this one included a free trip to Montreal along with entry in a tournament, so he had played. Incredibly he had placed in the top five and won the free trip. Smiling with excitement he sat up in bed.

"I was playing poker." She was just about to speak but he held up a finger, "Just listen please, I didn't lose any money. In fact this time I won $650 and even better a free trip to Montreal to play in a big tournament."

She smiled and kissed him on the forehead. "Well that is wonderful dear, taking anyone with you?"

"I've already e-mailed Cassandra and she'd love to go. It will be a nice romantic getaway for the two of us."

She replied, "I guess it's getting serious with you two. Make sure you don't get her pregnant!"

"Mom!" he cried out, even as a vampire his mom could still embarrass him.

"What, you think I don't know what you're doing with her?"

Relenting he nodded, *If only you knew what I was.* At least since he had started using spray-tan products at the business, he no longer had to worry about the health questions regarding his pale complexion. He replied, "I'll be careful. Oh and don't worry about your flight on Sunday. We fly out after yours, so it's no problem. I'll only be gone a few days so I'll get Vance to look after the cats."

She patted his knee and said, "I'll worry but I'm glad you'll have company. Just call us when you get there." His mom left the room and Joseph rubbed his temples, *my head, I'll sure be glad to sleep in the day again.*

Joseph glanced at the window, there was at least four feet of snow down. If he was human that would take him three hours or more and he would be exhausted as a vampire he could do it in a half hour and not even break a sweat, when it got dark. He smiled, *I am excited for Montreal, I was only there once before with friends and it will be nice to be there with Cassandra.* Getting dressed, he got out his iPad and checked his e-mail. One curious e-mail said "From Bill, please reply right away so we can chat"

He gulped as the reality of the Council and the coming battle came back to the front of his mind. He hadn't thought about the Council in over a month but it was time to face reality, it was part of the price for immortality as Cassandra had said. At least it was the good side, the right side. Opening the e-mail Joseph waited and within seconds a text appeared.

Joseph this is Bill, we are aware of recent events and we should talk. Cassandra has the connections to get your weapons through the airport. The tournament is a cover for the meeting. Get to Montreal Sunday afternoon and I'll send further instruction, stay safe.

Joseph replied, Understood, *see you in a couple of days.*

As with the Countess as soon as he replied all trace of the message and e-mail was gone. He sighed, "I should have known it was too good to be true. At least we don't have to deal with the Countess anymore." He then slapped his hand to his forehead. *Crap! I've already put on Facebook, Twitter and my blog that I won this tournament and will be going to Montreal. If the media finds out, well it won't be much of a secret that I'm gone. I hope that doesn't matter.*

* * *

Cassandra woke up in her new home on Logy Bay Road. She was almost done with her PhD in Women's Studies and she was tired of living in a dorm. The dorm room's purpose no longer mattered, as it helped her look like a normal student for Joseph. After that horrible night in November, they had grown closer. She hadn't heard from Anne but that was likely for the best. It meant her deception was working and they could prepare. They trained at least four times a week and dealt with criminals whenever they could find them. Joseph's idea of getting a police scanner app and driving around with it was a good one. Quickly they got to know all the areas where crimes usually happened and sometimes they even stopped them beforehand. She was done with lies and deception, well mostly. This house didn't count, it was an excellent surprise that Joseph would love. It was done in the shape of a castle and had a great view of the ocean. Now that Joseph had finished his degree and his parents had met her, she wanted him to move in with her. The fact that he still lived with his parents was sweet but it was time for him to be more independent.

She rubbed her smooth legs and let her hands drift up her body. Gently squeezing her nipples, she pictured Joseph, his hands on her, his lips kissing, his tongue exploring. It had taken months but the sex and the blood sharing had just gotten back to the level it was before he had asked her to leave that night. That had hurt her, but she hadn't asked for an apology, she had done wrong and was ready to move past it. Slipping her hand between her legs she moaned and gasped. She wanted him. She had made a compromise with him. While it couldn't compare to human blood, she had agreed to drink from a moose, or whatever animal Joseph found, once a week. There was no harm and it made him happy. She sent to him, *beloved. I want you in my blood and in my body, come and find me.*

His reply came instantly and while she felt excitement there was also nervous worry attached, *I'd love to fulfill your request but I need to tell you some important news.*

Cassandra sighed, getting out of bed she put her robe on. She turned her head towards the window, looking at the fresh, white snow. *Yes of course. You do know how to kill the mood sometimes.*

Oh…well sorry, this can't wait. Well the good news is we're going on a trip to Montreal and the bad news is it's to meet with the Council.

Her face feel into a deep frown and she immediately reached over to grasp her sword, her muscles tightening. *Goddamn bastards! Anne was supposed to be keeping them away from…*

Joseph cut her off, *oh I'm sorry, I meant Shatner and the good half of the Council. I should have made that clear, it's not bad news.*

Cassandra put her sword down and sat down on the bed, her shoulders relaxed and her hands stopped clenching. *Joseph! Tell me the important part first, I was already thinking the worst! A meeting with Bill is a good thing . . . I hope, they probably know what happened with the Countess. When do we leave?*

The reply was not as fast, she must have surprised him with her insight. *Right the Count…er Anne, yeah they might be a little upset over that. We leave Sunday, 5:30 at night. I couldn't help noticing you're not at your dorm room, care to share?*

It's a surprise, come out here and see. We'll talk about what's to come and maybe find a snack in the woods. First though I've got a hunger and it's for my sexy protégé.

The roads suck but I'll be there as soon as possible, I do love surprises.

Cassandra made herself some coffee, *I wonder who else is on this council? I've never met a President or a Prime Minister.*

* * *

"Be careful on your trip!" His Mom kissed and hugged him at the departure area of St. John's airport.

"I've gone to Montreal before and so has Cassandra, we'll be careful."

His dad came over and shook his hand, "Good luck, don't blow all the money you're worked hard to earn."

"I won't, you too have a safe trip and I'll talk to you soon."

They went into the airport and he suddenly got the strangest notion, it felt like he may never see them again. He shrugged it off, *I've just seen too many movies about plane crashes. Statistically flying is by far the safest way to travel and they're both in good health.*

He drove the car over to the employee parking lot and waited. He yawned and played with his phone. *Still hate up and about in the day, he rubbed his temples and squeezed his eyes shut. Cassandra's new house is incredible! A modern day castle and it's right on the ocean. Maybe when Mom and Dad get back from Florida I'll talk to them about moving out, it's getting harder to cover up what I am around all the time.*

As if that thought summoned her he felt Cassandra's presence. Turning he saw her red hair blowing in the wind.

The long tresses spilled out from the top of her white parka and her boots crunched on the ground as she walked. She smiled at him, he hit the button to open the trunk and then jumped out to open the door for her.

"Greetings beloved. Thank you, I do appreciate the chivalry on such a lousy day." She leaned over and kissed him quickly on the lips.

Joseph remembered that his cell phone was still bugged and thought to her, *what about my cell phone? It's still bugged, can we trust that only Anne listens to it now? Should I take it with me to Montreal?*

Cassandra squeezed his hand back and leaned against him, pressing her cold cheek to his to warm herself up. *You went to the airport to drop off your parents, so pretend you forgot it and just leave it in your car. Use the hotel phone to call your parents.*

Joseph scrunched up his face.

Oh Joseph don't be silly! I didn't read your thoughts, I've met your mother remember? I know she would want you to check in. Now let's get going okay?

Joseph nodded and moved the car. Before getting out, he made sure he had his wallet and put his phone in the glove box. He didn't like for Cassandra to pay for everything and he did have almost a grand on him from his poker winnings the past month. *Okay sorry, force of habit I guess. I assume you made arrangements to get our weapons on the plane?*

She nodded, "You know I did, you're not the only organized one." Joseph smiled as they entered the airport.

* * *

Green sat in his apartment, the hooker had fallen asleep. After three hours the coke had finally run out, snorting the lines off her ass and then letting her have the scraps. Four grams was usually not enough for two people. Laying his bottle of Coca-Cola down he rubbed the last of the coke around his gums and slid a finger across his phone. *Almost three, I'll check the news and crash. Darlene might be up for another fuck in morning.* Browsing social media something caught his attention. Jimmy had re-tweeted something from an idiot with the username "PokerStarNL" said he won a free trip to Montreal. He rubbed his eyes and clicked on the man's profile. *Joseph O'Reily, works at O'Reily Agencies, plays poker, D&D, avid TV watcher, Health nut, martial artist, vegetarian, gamer nut, agnostic.* "Holy shit that's him!" he exclaimed.

Darlene stirred, "Huh, Auggie, what is it babe? Some more blow show up?"

He smacked her ass, hard, "I told you not to call me that! No

there's no more blow! Get your lazy as to bed, I'll be there when I'm ready!"

She got up and pulled up her pants. "You didn't have to hit me so hard! If it wasn't snowing out I'd head home. Lousy fucking shit, I don't get paid enough..." her voice trailed off as she went upstairs.

He ignored her and studied the screen. "Yes I got you! Fucking stun ass told everyone where he is, or at least where he'll be. I'll just make some calls and find out when his flight gets back." He rubbed his hands together in excitement and found a last bit of coke that had fallen on the couch. Taking the last snort he jumped up in triumph, "Soon you shit-eating birdbrain I'll end your pitiful life. First to teach that ho a lesson, no one talks to me that way!"

He grabbed a broom handle and turned the music up so none of the neighbors would bother him, he gave Darlene a good beating. She wouldn't work for a few days. *No mistakes this time.* He hit Darlene in the stomach and on the back the fleshy parts that clothes could cover easy, *eight guys, guns, some bats, and a rifle, with any luck that whore redhead would be with him and I'll bury them both in woods.*

* * *

Joseph and Cassandra strolled around downtown Montreal, Joseph's stomach was in knots, but he was still happy to be here. Montreal was a cool city and he was here with Cassandra. She was hanging on his arm. He felt like an almost typical guy with his girlfriend going for a winter stroll. Here was even colder than Newfoundland, -35 with the wind chill, but with his powers on he didn't even shiver. It just meant almost empty streets and he liked it better than way, the city felt like it was his for the moment.

"That was great on the plane, you're better than ever," he whispered in her ear, "how was I?"

She nibbled on his ear playfully and breathed hot air in it. "Your tongue didn't quite hit the right spot most of the time but your blood is always delicious."

"Didn't hit the right spot...you certainly seemed to be enjoying yourself..." She smothered a giggle with her hand and he stopped walking, turning to her. "You're fucking with me, right?"

She smiled and kissed him on the cheek, "Of course I am beloved, just so easy sometimes. You know my body well, as I do yours. Your skills are better than ever."

Resuming their walk he laughed, "Yeah I guess I am an easy target some..."

Before he could to finish the sentence, Cassandra's phone beeped. She dug it out read the screen and held it up for Joseph to see, *we're all waiting on you. Finish your lovers stroll and head to the Queen Elizabeth Hotel on René-Lévesque Boulevard, we'll be in the penthouse suite. Bill.*

Joseph gulped, "Well that didn't last long. I guess we should get this over with."

She squeezed his hand. "It'll be fine, you're strong and can handle it. Besides I'm anxious to see who else is on the better half of the Council."

They both picked up the pace and soon found themselves at the hotel. In the bottom window just before the entrance was a white bed that had a sign "Bed-in 1969." Joseph studied it for a moment as his breath puffed out in front of him, something he always did when out in public to avoid suspicion.

Joseph snapped his fingers, "Ahh I get it, this must be one of the places John and Yoko did a protest for the Vietnam War. It's a nice coincidence Bill picked here."

Cassandra scrapped a little ice off the window with her fingernails. "It may be no coincidence at all, Bill may have met one or both of them, he was born in Montreal after all."

Joseph smiled and said, "Look at you! Doing research and everything. I guess soon you'll be quoting Star Trek lines." She punched him playfully in the shoulder, "You wish, now let's get going. I sense six vampires upstairs."

They entered the building and made their way to the penthouse floor. Joseph opened the door, his heart in his mouth and his stomach twisted and full of butterflies. The room was brightly lit and Joseph turned his head from side to side, gaining awareness of his surroundings. Just inside the door was a man, he didn't carry any weapons and smiled at them. He held his arms out in front of them, "May I take your coats and weapons Madame and Monsieur? Mr. Shatner promises no harm will come to you here." His French accent was thick. Joseph shrugged and then did as was asked. *In for a penny in for a pound*, he sent to Cassandra.

They made their way to an adjoining room. Tasteful decorations of grey and purple along with statues and paintings adorned the walls, all of which barely registered in Joseph's mind as the men who lined the two couches inside came into view. If Joseph's jaw could have hit the floor it would have. He turned his head slightly, Cassandra's eyes wide open, shock evident and stared straight ahead. Joseph's hands fell limp at his sides as one by one James Oliver Rigney, Jr., Barack Obama, Leonardo da Vinci, Larry King and Keith Richards stood up. Bill Shatner was already standing by the couch on the right, a drink in one hand.

Cassandra gathered herself a little more quickly, "Mr. President, Mr. da Vinci, Mr. King, Mr. Richards, a pleasure to meet you all and Mr. Shatner, lovely to see you again." She did a slight curtsey and they all came over in turn to shake her hand. James Rigney introduced himself to her.

Joseph was still awestruck. *He's alive*, he wanted to scream, *and Keith Richard is a vampire and...* All of these thoughts ended as President Obama came over to him and extended his hand. "It's a pleasure to meet you son. Now I know this is a little much for you to take in all at once but we're all on the same team here."

Rigney took a more direct approach. He charged over, pushed Obama out of the way, and slammed a fist into Joseph's gut, making him double over with pain.

"You stupid ignoramus! You could have ruined everything and killed us all with your little stunt!" Shatner quickly stepped forward to separate the two of them.

"Goddamn it James, I'm mad at the little shit too but we're above this! Let's all sit down and discuss this like civilized people, agreed?" The rest of them nodded and Cassandra, who had instinctively reached for her sword that wasn't there, sat down in an empty chair. Joseph coughed and held his stomach for a moment, the pain quickly faded and he sat down, his face red with embarrassment. *One of my favorite authors and that's what he thinks of me*, his face fell.

Bill was the last to sit down. "I must apologize for James' actions, he is one of the more emotional members. I know you're brimming with questions and once business is out of the way some will be answered. For now, we must discuss what happened in St. Pierre. You made a very risky decision and fortunately for us and the world, you may have made the right one."

Joseph's mind was racing and he tried to clear his head. *Rigney here, alive and he punched me and the President and…*

Cassandra entered his mind, *focus darling. The time for hero worship and awe will come later. For now, this is serious.*

Joseph reached over to a table next to him and picked up a glass of water, taking a big gulp of it. He steadied himself and looked to Shatner. "We only learned of the Countess' replacement a few days ago, which means your plan has worked. Anne seems to have fooled all of the other council members, except the Count who she has managed to avoid so far. Why did you act so rashly? Why did you need to kill the Countess so soon and without telling us? The plan itself was a good one, but if you had just notified us we could have helped." Bill took a big drink of whiskey and peered over the rip of the glass. His eyes filled with judgment that Joseph felt. "If you had told us then maybe four people wouldn't have died. They were just doing their jobs, perhaps even brainwashed by the Countess."

Joseph raised his hand, he felt like he was in some kind of dream and he wasn't sure if it was a bad one or not. He also recognized that he had a right to explain himself and waited for someone to spot his hand. Obama did, "Speak young man, we're ready to hear your side of the story."

Joseph cleared his throat and started, "Well…umm it was Anne who first mentioned the idea to me. She felt that the Countess could not resist the opportunity to bring her into the fold. Anne felt, and all of us later agreed, that this was the time to strike down one of our foes; a pre-emptive strike. I apologize for not contacting you Mr. Shatner, but we didn't know how long the Countess would have the ring on and that was essential for the plan to work. I'll also add that the Countess had just sent two vampires to scare my friend and beat the crap out of me, I was pissed off."

Rigney spoke. His voice was rough and gravely, but not without some interest, "I do understand your anger, that half of the Council has pushed us all around for too long. You speak of the ring that hides our presence from another, correct? You have learned of some other property it possesses?"

This time it was Cassandra who responded. She crossed her legs and leaned forward, "I'm sure Joseph won't mind if I tell this part. While I was in Paris making vampires for the Countess I asked her some questions that revealed more about this ring. With it, you're not only undetectable by other vampires, your telepathy is also cut off, including all communication with your sire and I assume any younglings you have made."

Rigney nodded as did Shatner, Richards sipped on his drink and Obama leaned forward, listening intently. Cassandra looked to each of them and then back to Rigney, "The ring is addictive to wear. I saw the Countess stare at it many times and touch it. She seemed unable to take it off."

This time King answered, "This is very interesting. We all saw the ring and watched the Emperor give it to the Countess. Perhaps he wanted to be rid of the addictive quality and drawbacks it possesses. You both made certain she did not contact the Count or anyone else during the fight?"

Joseph nodded and replied, "Yes Mr. King, when the fight was over she still had it on. On the hand she had left that is."

King nodded at this and Shatner scrunched up his face. "The Countess, despite whatever else she did, was an incredible swordsman. I ask because of a few more concerns about this spy you have put in place."

Cassandra looked to Joseph and then towards King, "I get the feeling neither of us is going to like what comes next."

This time it was Rigney who spoke up. His face was a little more relaxed but his voice was still clipped, "We'll just have to hope Anne can keep avoiding the Count or be good at her part should they meet. The Count someone likely to discover this deception and you'd better hope he doesn't."

Joseph gulped and looked to Cassandra, *he is only trying to scare us, he's afraid too and is covering.*

Joseph put on a small grin, *good point. He is kind of a jerk.*

Rigney looked between the two, pushed his eyebrows together and continued, "How has Anne deceived people in the Council so well? Aside from her appearance, her performance, from the video we saw, was nothing short of perfect."

Joseph straightened in his chair. "Well…it…we had to do something I'm not proud of. When Anne and Cassandra had her near death, we all forced her into an embrace. With all three of us pressing into her weakened mind we learned…everything. Every last gory detail and memory was revealed so that Anne could answer any question or act in any way that was needed."

All of the other men present had wide eyes. Rigney cleared his throat and Richards had another big swig of his drink. Da Vinci turned to face Joseph, "That is…well unpleasant and a horrible thing to do, even to the Countess. I must admit though, a brilliant idea and one none of us ever thought of. It does certainly explain why it took so long for us to find the truth and with any luck the other members' never will." They all nodded slowly and Joseph knew their eyes settled upon him. While he felt some had a grudging respect, others stared in judgment, almost in horror.

Joseph averted his eyes. Thankfully, before the moment became ever more unbearable da Vinci continued, "The other problem is Black Bart, the pirate who created Anne. He's still alive and would almost certainly be able to tell who the Countess is. You and Cassandra will have to eliminate him. We have decided you're the ones best suited to the task. We'll let you know when it's a good time. We won't order you to do this, but I hope you'll volunteer as you do have an aptitude for killing."

Everyone else nodded and Joseph gulped. Cassandra turned to him with her dark, hypnotic eyes meeting his. She sent to him, *he will be one less thing to worry about when the battle comes.*

Joseph frowned but steeled himself, *I do know what Bart did and I know he could ruin everything. They're right it's a loose end that has to be tied up. It's time for me to trust Bill and all these good vampires.* "I will do it Mr. da Vinci," he said, "and I know Cassandra will also, just let us know when and where."

Leonardo smiled and nodded. "Excellent, you're strong for someone so young and have a good heart. My friends call me the Master, I would like it if you both did as well. All the news tonight is not so grim, I am perfecting a robot dog that will protect us and kill those we oppose. Also, each of you please take these cell phones. They're completely untraceable and altered to work for each of you only. Simply say any of our names and it will connect you to that person. It will even suppress any other listening device that may be nearby."

Leonardo handed them the phones. Joseph turned to Cassandra in time as she produced a small smile and a nod, her thoughts entered his mind with warmth and pride, *you're a strong warrior with character and morality. Whatever may come we will face it together.*

Joseph let out a massive sigh and as the door opened. The butler came into the room and had a tray of drinks. Joseph took a beer and had a long chug from it, there was a weight off his shoulders with everything out in the open. Each of the others did the same. Shatner stood and moved towards Joseph, "We're not sure when the Emperor and his cronies will strike, but we all agree it will be sometime this year. Until then, wait for us to contact you." They all started to move about the room now, some using their phones and others chatting with each other. Joseph finished off his beer and Shatner offered him another.

Joseph took another swig, he would like to get at least a little drunk after everything he had discovered tonight. Shatner also started working on a second drink, "With all that business taken care of you must have lots of questions. We're all here for a little longer so feel free to ask a few." Cassandra had started chatting with Keith Richards. Joseph extended his hand and Shatner took it in a firm grim. "All right thanks, and I am sorry for not informing you of our plan."

Shatner grinned, releasing his hand and leaned in close. "You're got guts Joseph, Cassandra too. I'll give you both that."

Joseph smiled broadly, *that's more like it. Bill thinks I have guts, excellent!* "I do have a few questions if you don't mind. How exactly do these dogs work?"

Shatner smiled and motioned to Da Vinci, "You'll need to speak to the Master on his dogs of war." The Master came over next to the two of them.

"Master if I could trouble you, these robot dogs. Do they have flesh and fur over the metal and sentience to some degree?"

The Master smiled and responded enthusiastically, "No they're not meant to infiltrate, just to destroy the Emperor's forces and yes they have some intelligence. I have a lab in Hawaii, perhaps you both will visit sometime, once Bart is dealt with."

Joseph beamed from ear to ear, "I would love that and I'm sure Cassandra would too. Thank you so much."

Barack Obama came over to join the conversation, "Let me tell you these dogs have bark and bite! I helped test out one of them and it damn near killed me. I'd be happy to have you both over at the vacation house in Hawaii. I could figure out a reason to explain you both."

Cassandra came over and put her arm through Joseph's, "Thank you Mr. President, we would be honored to join both of you. While I'm certain Joseph here could talk your ear off I think we should be going. You all have important duties to attend to I'm certain."

Obama smiled at both of them, "No point arguing with the lady. I should get back to the capital. Joseph, Cassandra, a pleasure to meet you both. The next time I see you may not be so pleasant but I promise you old Teddy still has lots of fight left in him."

Joseph pushed his eyebrows together and squinted. *Old Teddy? What does that mean?*

Cassandra entered his mind, *Obama has probably portrayed other political figures, possibly other presidents. Don't worry I will tell you everything Keith said. We should leave now, we don't want to wear out our welcome.*

Joseph sighed, *All right. At least we can contact any of them now If need be.* He went around and shook everyone's hand. Joseph had to speak with Richards, "I love the Stones, I saw you guys in Toronto a few years ago and you put on a hell of a show."

Richards let go of his hand and clapped him on the shoulder, "Thanks chap, it's what I do. Hit me up for some front row seats anytime. We'll be on tour later this year."

Joseph also went over to James Rigney, "I just wanted to say how much I loved your *Wheel of Time* books. Will you do any more writing?"

Rigney shook his hand firmly. "Sorry about hitting you before but it was a foolhardy move. Thanks for that, I am happy with the way it ended. I am taking a break from writing but who knows what the future may bring. You'll find my influence on other people you have enjoyed, Stevenson and Hemingway namely."

Joseph's eyes opened wide, his smiled pulled hard at the corners of his mouth and he stammered, "You're welcome…other people you mean you're…err you've . . ., well that's wonderful! I can never thank you enough!"

Rigney laughed a little, "You're welcome my boy, remember to get out there and experience life, that's always the best advice I could give."

Cassandra came over and nudged Joseph in the ribs adding, "Thank you Mr. Rigney, I'm sure you've given Joseph plenty to think about." Rigney nodded and smiled, slipping away. Joseph got the hint and turned with Cassandra, heading towards the door.

Shatner came over to both of them as they exited the room, "The rest will leave shortly. You probably have a month or so before Bart can be eliminated, enjoy the time but be vigilant. I have to tell you one last thing, since Anne has all of the Countess' memories and is acting as her, there is a concern. The possibly that she will lose herself and truly become another Countess. With that of course means a horrible possibility…"

Cassandra finished the sentence, "Of a threat to be eliminated. Mr. Shatner, I speak for all of us when I say I hope it doesn't come to that. But if it does…well as you said, we started it."

Bill nodded and shook Joseph's hand. He gave Cassandra a hug and kissed her hand. "Your wisdom is only matched by your sense of duty. Joseph, please do keep in touch. My apologies for ending the meeting on such a sour note but you needed to know. Enjoy the rest of your time in the city and there is actually a poker tournament tomorrow, the entry you have is real."

Joseph smiled at that. *Some poker would be nice before we go back.* "Yes Mr. Shatner I may just do that and thank you."

Shatner simply nodded and closed the door. Cassandra leaned against Joseph's shoulder and they walked toward the elevator. "That wasn't so bad. As usual, we'll deal with the future when it comes, and now we know we have all of these people are on our side, feels good."

Joseph nodded, "Easy for you say, you didn't get punched in the stomach!" He hit the button for the elevator.

Cassandra raised an eyebrow at him, "Unless you want to have it happen again I'd watch it. You and Anne did come up with this plan, I always knew there would be consequences. I'd say you got off easy." Cassandra walked into the elevator and Joseph followed.

Joseph held up his hands. "Yeah, okay I agree. I was lucky, I guess it could have gone much worse." He pushed the button for the ground floor. "Teddy, he called himself Teddy. I got it!" He snapped his fingers. "Obama used to be Teddy Roosevelt! That is cool, Teddy was a fierce fighter." He smiled and held out his hand, Cassandra interlaced her fingers with his.

Y"I do mostly feel better. I'd like to go to the cobblestone square I was at last year with my friends for a while and some hotel sex later I hope."

She licked his ear and whispered, "My horny devil, both sound good to me." Joseph smiled and they walked out onto the street once more. *Stevenson and Hemingway! Could Rigney have lived as even more writers? It certainly makes reading everything they've even done an exciting adventure.* It was after midnight and the streets as quiet as a tomb. Snow swirled around them, two lovers in a dangerous time.

Chapter 18: Green's Revenge

Joseph held onto Cassandra's hand as the plane neared St. John's airport. It was Tuesday around eleven at night and Joseph smiled to himself, the unpleasantness of the Council meeting almost forgotten. Here in Newfoundland another March snowstorm. Joseph could clearly remember a day in April where they got over one-hundred centimeters. Montreal was a lot of fun: the restaurants; the Eagles concert; and of course the poker tournament. He came second and won ten grand. It was a massive thrill. He could have took first but didn't want to draw too much attention to himself. Joseph put on his headphones and listened to an appropriate song…

Some things in life are bad, they can really make you mad, other things just make you swear and curse

Cassandra entered his mind, *not upset about the snow beloved?*

"Always look on the bright side of life," he couldn't whistle but he loved this song, it always made him feel better. He smiled and stopped the music realizing he was singing aloud.

"Most of the time I would be, but tonight I'm in a good mood. I'm happy to be with you and I'd like to move in with you in a few months, if that's ok. Winter is almost done, I hope, and after that massive poker win, I thought we might plan a trip somewhere warm. Hawaii would be a lot of fun."

She leaned over and kissed him fiercely, "Wonderful idea, I just need a few weeks to finish up my thesis and make arrangements for the house. Of course I'd love you to have you in my castle, June would be nice treat for your birthday too. Would you like to give me some of your money to invest?"

The plane shook with turbulence and the lights flicked. Joseph didn't mind flying but this was starting to bother him. Vampire or not he didn't want to be in a plane crash. Joseph nodded and handed Cassandra a thousand bucks. The pilot announced over the loudspeaker, "Going to be a bumpy landing, fasten your seat belts and hold on."

Joseph let go of Cassandra's hand and gripped the hand rests. "Try to relax beloved, I sense the ground. The pilot wouldn't land if it wasn't safe and besides, you could damage the seats and that grand you gave me will be gone."

Joseph chuckled a little at that. Cassandra always helped to take his mind off what troubled him and helped lighted his mood. He caressed her long red hair and stroked her face. "You're quite a woman you know? Have I told you that lately?"

She smiled back as the plane touched down, "Well you know the saying, flattery will get you everywhere."

The pilot came over the loudspeaker, "Welcome to St. John's. The temperature is currently minus one and the weather, well you can look outside, it's bad."

Joseph let out a sigh, "Well that's a relief. As usual you're right."

Cassandra smiled, "I'm a woman, kind of our thing."

* * *

Cassandra put her overnight bag in the trunk.

"You're never going to get the car out of here. We'll go to my place, it will be a slog but we'll go right through…" A bullet streaked through the air and struck the back car tire, narrowly missing Cassandra's leg and Joseph's foot, cutting her off short. Cassandra instantly charged towards some nearby trees where the shot came from.

Joseph, despite all his training and his fights, was shocked. He instantly reached out with his senses, but aside from Cassandra no other vampires here, not within miles at least. His hesitation cost him as another bullet streaked through the night, this one went through his side and into the trunk. He cried out "Fuck me!" as blood spurted and landed on the snow. Now he had to act. Getting under the car, he crawled to the other side as another bullet smashed the driver's side window. He got back to the trunk and got his sword, ducking as another shot whizzed overhead. He drew his sword and started to move in Cassandra's direction. The snow swirled around him and whipped in his face like sand, but with vampire vision it made no difference. He was slowed, but still moving as another bullet zipped by, this one taking off the top of his ear. Blood once more flew into the air and a few drops fell to the ground in the snow.

There was shouting and soon he saw the source. No less than eight guys charged out of the woods and Cassandra screamed in his mind, *Joseph! Leap the remaining distance, get here now!* Cassandra drew her sword and the men stopped just for a second. It was all the time he needed as yet another bullet streaked through the air, this one tearing at his right side. He was already running and made a huge leap. His leg screamed in protest, but he made it work. His side burned as well, but he gritted his teeth against the pain. He sailed through the air a good fifty feet or more, the farthest he had ever jumped.

Joseph heard a man yell out, "You bunch of pussies! There's eight of us and two of them! I don't care if she has a fucking sword, just bash their heads in!" As the burliest man, at least six-foot-four came forward carrying a large wooden bat, Cassandra moved into action. She sheared the bat in half and then shifted behind him, the second cut dug a deep gash in his back causing him to double over with the pain, she moved quicker than any human.

Joseph landed on top of two of the men, knocking them to the ground. They had certainly not expected someone to leap at them from so far away. Joseph never gave them a chance to recover, he kicked one in the chest and heard several loud snaps. The second managed to get to his knees as Joseph whirled back, the hilt of his sword slamming down on the man's head, sticking into his skull and killing him instantly. With his sword stuck in the man's head, two of the other swung at him. They had steel pipes and they connected painfully. The first one landed across his back and the other smashed into his jaw, breaking off two teeth and causing blood to spray out.

Joseph's vision swam. In double and triples he could still make out Cassandra. She moved fluidly and kicked one man hard in the groin, then turned and stabbed another clean through the chest. To make matters worse, there was still the shooter. Joseph had some cover with the men but Cassandra was more exposed. A shot took three of her fingers off and caused her to drop her weapon. The wounds on Joseph hurt, but without silver bullets, they healed quickly. His head cleared enough for him to reach out and grab a steel rod as it moved toward his head. He turned and flipped behind the man, using him for cover. Another man struck Joseph's cover with a pipe, a solid crack on his skull caused the man to fall unconscious. Joseph grabbed the pipe and shoved the unconscious man forward with a kick. Joseph went to work, he had spent years training with sticks. Once more, two men struck at him, Joseph ducked under one and smashed into his side, this time causing blood, bone and flesh to explode outward onto the snow. Not slowing down, he stripped the dying man of his own weapon, a crowbar, and used a weapon in each hand. Bones broke, another head was smashed in, blood continued to fall on the snow and soon just two remained. Joseph had lost all thought now, he was a creature of death and instinct and screamed out, "I'll kill every goddamn one of you!"

Cassandra had issues of her own, the rifle went off again and this time got her in the back. She screamed once more with the pain but continued to move. Her own sword was covered up already with the snow but Joseph's was hard to miss, sticking out of a dead man's head. She rolled on the ground and quickly reached it. With a disgusting crunch, she wrestled it free and sliced at the last two men trying to run away. She took off the leg of one of them and pouncing like a cat, impaled the second.

Joseph saw just left one man on the ground, he rolled around and moaned, obviously no threat. He scanned about and found the shooter. A man lay on top of a large branch in a tree some twenty feet up. He wore a white coat and had some kind of military issued sniper rifle. While some of his face was covered by the sight, Joseph still managed to recognize him, it was that man they had beat up by the church back in October, the pimp. Joseph's eyes opened wide with shock, "Green? You...you fucking piece of crap! We let you live and you do this?"

Joseph reached behind for the gun normally tucked in his pants but it wasn't there, *still in the trunk of the car, fuck*! A bullet shell fell to the ground as Green pulled back the bolt and steadied his aim, his finger on the trigger. "You bet your fucking ass it's me dick brain! I saved the one with the explosive tip just for you and the whore with you." He slammed the bullet in place and pulled back the bolt, and slammed it in place, putting another bullet in his teeth.

The Newfoundland Vampire   Charles O'Keefe

At that moment, Joseph knew it was over. He knew that in the end it wasn't his training, his powers or his fighting skills that had failed him, not even Cassandra, it was his own nature, his mercy. That night he had taken pity on Green, even though he was a murderous piece of shit Joseph had left him alive. He sent to Cassandra, *I love you, kill this bastard for me and tell my parents I loved them. Whatever the cops did with this son of bitch wasn't enough as he's...*Whatever that last thought was, was cut off as the bullet streaked towards him and half of Joseph's head exploded.

* * *

Cassandra felt it, Joseph was in terrible danger. She had just impaled one of those goons into the snow and turned. She turned her head up into the trees and saw him, Green, the bastard they should have taken care of last year. He blended in the snow, all in some white camo suit and had a larger rifle propped up against his shoulder. She broke into a run but it was too late. He aimed, put a bullet in the chamber from his pocket and chambered the bolt. She heard Joseph's thought in her mind, felt his love mixed with an unbearable sadness, someone who knew they were going to die. *I love you, kill this bastard for me and tell my parents I loved them. Whatever the cops did with this son of bitch wasn't enough as he's* . . . Green pulled the trigger and Joseph, her beloved, her last true descendant and best friend's presence winked out as half his head exploded out onto the snow.

Green put the other bullet in the chamber, fixed the bolt and screamed out, "Finally! Lousy shit, who's laughing now?"

Cassandra knew only rage and sadness, she let out an air-splitting scream, "NOO!" and Green had to cover his ears. She wanted his eardrums to burst, she didn't care who heard. Tears filled her eyes but she blinked them away, immediately weaving from side to side, seeing what the last bullet could do, *son of bitch has some kind of explosive top, it won't be worth a damn against me though!*

A man that she thought was dead managed to get up on one elbow and take a shot at her. The deep snow was slowing her down and she felt an immense pain as the bullet pierced her heart. She gasped and gripped her chest for a moment, soon realizing she wasn't dead. She snarled at him, *not wood, you'll have to do better than that your miserable turd!* She flung her sword at him, in went right through his back, impaling him and the gun fell limp from his hand. Looking up she saw the smile disappear from Green's face, he turned pale and it was her turn to smile. Her eyes lit up red and her fangs came down. She watched him blink and rub at his eyes, wanting to savor the moment she listened in on his thoughts, *what the fuck! How can she be human? Is she a terminator or some shit?* Green looked back to her, aimed and took his last shot but missed and as Cassandra tensed her legs muscles and leaped into the air. Cassandra was airborne and watched Green drop the rifle and draw a handgun, too late, she thought, she slammed into him and wrapped her arms around his chest, wrenching him from his post and landing on him as they feel to the ground.

"Ahh fuck!" he screamed as he tumbled down. When he landed the wind was knocked out of him and he couldn't breathe. She gripped his hand, the same hand that Joseph broke before, and this time crushed it completely.

He tried to yell but only managed to spit blood at her. Cassandra ripped off his coat and shirt, tearing at his skin with her nails and drawing blood. She got off him for a second, drawing back her fist, ready for a blow that would cave his skull in completely. She felt the bullet in her chest get pushed out and the wound seal up.

Green managed to choke out, "I'll see you in hell, you fucking cunt! Right where…" He doesn't deserve a quick death, I'll break every bone and keep him awake, severe tendons, cut open veins, reseal them with my blood, I can make it go on for hours, for now I'll make him shup up. His last words cut off she punched him in the face, holding in her rage, and he fell unconscious.

It can't be! Not after all we've gone through, not after us finding our way back to each other. Not some fucking pimp and his cronies take Joseph out! She had broken Green's hand, arm, all the bones in his face, and had torn open his chest with her fingernails just for spite. Her fury on this Green man was almost beyond description. Her fangs just inches from his throat and she was about to open the jugular, tears rolled down her face and her only comfort was that at least she could fulfill Joseph's wish. She could kill Green and find Joseph's parents in Florida. Then something stopped her. A tickle at the back of her mind, a memory and an idea mixed together and gave her hope.

"John!" she exclaimed, leaving Green on the ground. "He was shot in the head but it didn't matter, he was a vampire and he lived." Reaching out with her mind she felt for Joseph's presence but it wasn't there. Blood and brains still oozed from his skull. She wiped away her tears and concentrated. "Blood!" she cried out, "This fucker's blood will do some good after all!" She carried Green's limp body over to Joseph. She gently opened Joseph's mouth and bit Green's jugular, the blood started to pump out. At first it didn't work, blood just filled Joseph's mouth and dribbled back out. Then she carefully tilted his head back and tried again, the blood ran down his throat. The blood from his skull had stopped its flow. His brain stopped oozing out, it stayed in place. She gathered up all the bodies, some barely alive, and she stacked them nearby. She felt Green's heart stop. Cassandra saw a flash, maybe it was just her imagination, but she could have sworn she saw a flash of red in Joseph's eyes.

"Live! Goddammit, live! I've sacrificed too much!" She sent to Joseph, *you have strength, use it dammit! You deserve to live, I love you more than anything, you are the only connection I have left to this world! Have all this blood. Have mine too, LIVE!*" She opened up the throats of the remaining men and held each one to his mouth. Some more blood came out of them and went down Joseph's throat. This time it wasn't her imagination. Joseph's fangs came down, just a little, but enough for him to bite. She tore her coat away from her neck and used her nails to open a vein. She pressed her throat to his mouth and felt his fangs sink in. Just a tiny bit at first. Tears continued to roll down her face. His grip grew stronger and his skull began to close over. She cried and laughed with happiness. Reaching out with her senses she now found something. It wasn't Joseph's mind, but it was a presence and it was in him. All the blood had did it. He was alive and would recover. Cassandra carefully removed his fangs and sealed up the wounds. Wrapping his head in a cloth she tore off her coat and carried him away on her shoulder. Somehow she managed to get her phone out and hit the number, "Big cl-clean up by St. John's Airport. Bring everyone you have right . . . now" *That was one number I'll never forget, used it to clean up Donald's mess last year and sadly it may not be the last time.* She had lost so much blood had given so much to Joseph it was all she could do to put one foot in front of the other.

Slowly, she forced herself on. She wanted to surprise Joseph with a stable on the back of her property. Now the horses would have to serve another purpose, they would ensure both their survival and give them the strength to live, the strength to love and the will to carry on.

Chapter 19: Every little thing he does is magic

Leonardo da Vinci stroked his long beard and started at the metal walls of his lab. *Unfortunate that none of my companions know the truth. I was there at the beginning; I made Commodus and am the creator of vampires. I have given him almost two-thousand years to change, to show a glimmer of the humanity that I know he once possessed, but it is all gone.* He pressed some buttons on his phone, making sure for the tenth time today no one approached from above ground.

He was my emperor, he was almost like a god to me, something I worshiped and adored. I used all my skill in magic. Called to all the gods I knew then as a philosopher and sorcerer. Called to any who might help and help they did but at what price?

He closed his eyes and reached out with his senses, Obama's presence was fading, now over a mile away. *The Emperor made a fatal flaw the night he killed me. He kissed me on the lips, with blood still on his. So new was the magic that somehow that tiny bit of his blood restored me, gave me eternal life as well. My birth was long and painful, days before I could even stand but the past is gone and I must focus on the future.* He looked down at the metal work table. The war dog lay in pieces on it but the real animals in the secret compartment had beating hearts and bodies full of blood. *A shame that I must sacrifice even more in pursuit of the ritual but Commodus must be stopped.*

Pressing a hidden panel on the wall, a door slid open to reveal a pen with goats and another room off to the side. *The magic I could once wield with ease is so much harder now, perhaps due that to fact I am no longer human.* He walked into the room and took the rope tied to the goat, undoing the knotted end attached to the wall. The goat protested, perhaps somehow sensing what was to come, but Galen simply picked it up and carried it to the other side. In this room there was a drain, a large pentagram scrawled in blood on the floor and three other goats all tied with ropes to rings on the wall. The names "Aeternitas", "Apollo" and "Ntevorta" painted on the floor in blood. *Eternity, poetry, music and the future, all elements needed here. There is a kind of art in creating this spell and they will help their long-suffering servant. So many gods I've called on, so much blood. I've done this thousands of times.*

Tying the goat to the drain in the center he closed his eyes and concentrated. Obama was gone, he could no longer feel his presence. Reaching into the folds of his robe he pulled out an iPhone. Activating the security app he made certain there was no one around the park, the heat sensing cameras only picked up small animals. He picked a song and put the phone back in his pocket. The music would help him concentrate and speak to Apollo. He drew a dagger from his belt and began the ghastly work of killing the goats and eviscerating them.

The goat screamed once as Galen slit its throat and the blood begin to move towards the drain. Moving around the room he killed each goat as mercifully and swiftly as he could. Dipping his hands in the blood he traced the pentagram once more and then the names of each god.

The more gruesome part of spreading the intensities around the pentagram began and Galen increased his speed. *Time, I must show the gods my own mastery over time, show them the opposite of what I want to happen.* Finally he called out in a loud voice "I call on thee Aeternitas, Apollo and Ntevorta, stop the flow of time for but a moment. Give me the chance I need to defeat him and save this world from darkness, this I beg as your faithful servant." The music continued as he felt the magic flow around him and time slowed down…

There will be miracles, after the last war is won

The Newfoundland Vampire   Charles O'Keefe

The music abruptly stopped and he knew it had worked. After all this time he had done it. To make certain, he jumped back and flung the dagger from his hand. As he had hoped, the blade moved only a few inches and stopped in mid-air. Quickly switching to the security app, his eyes opened wide and his mouth turned into a large smile, a mouse was frozen in mid-step and a bird was caught in mid-flight directly above this spot. He fell to his knees and began to weep with pleasure and relief as the knife continued its journey and banged off the wall on the other side of the room. The bird flew on through the night and the mouse scurried away. Time had stopped but he had not. It was only perhaps ten seconds, but enough for what is needed. He quickly licked his hands clean and retrieved his notebook. He wrote all the details furiously. He still had much work to do. The magic had to be imbued into an item he could smash to activate. Smiling and laughing to himself, he got a bucket of water and began to clean the mess of the ritual room.

"You're strong and have magic, but you will not win the battle to come. I will take back those items you stole from me and the future this planet deserves will come to pass." Blood ran down into the drain as Galen continued to clean. *It wasn't all for nothing, I have performed a small miracle that I hope will save us all.*

###

~ABOUT THE AUTHOR~

Charles O'Keefe lives in the beautiful province of Newfoundland, Canada, with his wife and two feline 'children,' Jude and Eleanor. He is a part-owner of a beauty wholesale business enjoys many hobbies and activities that include writing, reading, watching fantasy/science-fiction movies and television shows, gaming, poker, walking, Pilates, martial arts, Dungeons and Dragons and of course fantasizing about vampires.

To find out more about Charles, go to Twitter and Facebook or visit his web site.

http://www.charlesokeefe.com/